Praise for R

'Jahn just gets better and better. He's a writer not to be missed'   **Mark Billingham**

'Dark, compelling and powerful . . . a rare and fine talent'
R. J. Ellory

'*The Dispatcher*, which reads at a cracking pace, is a one-sitting, fist-in-mouth read'   *Guardian*

'Reminiscent of Cormac McCarthy's tales of vengeance, *The Dispatcher* is an impressively accomplished perform-ance that never strains for mythic power but nevertheless acquires it'   *Sunday Times*

'Armed with a seat-of-the-pants plot that takes some au-dacious risks and prose that proved gritty and gruelling, Jahn has produced a thriller with a steely death-grip. I walked into a tree reading it; no greater recommendation needed'   *Financial Times*

'*The Last Tomorrow* is Jahn's most ambitious and complex novel to date . . . Murder, blackmail, execution and betrayal – of one's own integrity and morality – stalk this very fine, multi-layered novel'   Book of the Week, ***Daily Mirror***

THE GENTLE ASSASSIN

Ryan David Jahn lives in Louisville, Kentucky, with his wife Jessica and two beautiful little girls, Francine and Matilda. His novels include *Acts of Violence*, which won the Crime Writers' Association John Creasey Dagger, *Low Life*, *The Dispatcher* and *The Last Tomorrow*. His work has been translated into twelve languages.

Visit his website at www.ryandavidjahn.com
Or follow him on Twitter @ RyanDavidJahn

By Ryan David Jahn

ACTS OF VIOLENCE

LOW LIFE

THE DISPATCHER

THE LAST TOMORROW

THE GENTLE ASSASSIN

RYAN DAVID JAHN

THE GENTLE ASSASSIN

PAN BOOKS

First published 2014 by Pan Books,
an imprint of Pan Macmillan, a division of Macmillan Publishers Limited
Pan Macmillan, 20 New Wharf Road, London N1 9RR
Basingstoke and Oxford
Associated companies throughout the world
www.panmacmillan.com

ISBN 978-0-230-75755-4

1 3 5 7 9 8 6 4 2

A CIP catalogue record for this book is available from the British Library.

Typeset by Ellipsis Digital Limited, Glasgow
Printed and bound by CPI Group (UK) Ltd, Croydon, CR0 4YY

Visit www.panmacmillan.com to read more about all our books
and to buy them. You will also find features, author interviews and
news of any author events, and you can sign up for e-newsletters
so that you're always first to hear about our new releases.

For Jessica Alt Jahn –

The destination I didn't even know
I was traveling toward.

You make every day
worth it.

Assassination is a term thought to be derived from 'hash-ish', a drug similar to marijuana, said to have been used by Hasan-ibn-Sabah to induce motivation in his followers, who were assigned to carry out political and other murders, usually at the cost of their lives.

It is here used to describe the planned killing of a person who is not under the legal jurisdiction of the killer, who is not physically in the hands of the killer, who has been selected by a resistance organization or person for death, and whose death provides positive advantages to that organization or person.

Assassination is an extreme measure not normally used in clandestine operations. It should be assumed that it will never be ordered or authorized by any U.S. Head-quarters, though the latter may in rare instances agree to its execution by members of an associated foreign service. This reticence is partly due to the necessity for committing communications to paper. No assassination instructions should ever be written or recorded. Consequently, the decision to employ this technique must nearly always be reached in the field, at the area where the act will take place. Decision and instructions should be confined to an absolute minimum of persons. Ideally, only one person will be involved. No report may be made, but usually the act will be properly covered by normal news services, whose output is available to all concerned.

Murder is not morally justifiable. Self-defense may be argued if the victim has knowledge which may destroy the resistance organization or person if divulged. Assassination of persons responsible for atrocities or reprisals may be regarded as just punishment. Killing a political leader whose burgeoning career is a clear and present danger to the cause of freedom may be held necessary.

But assassination can seldom be employed with a clear conscience. Persons who are morally squeamish should not attempt it.

PART ONE

SHED

To most men the death of his
father is a new lease of life.
Samuel Butler

THEN:

He pulls the 1963 Chevy Impala to the curb and kills the engine before looking toward the rearview mirror. A police car grows larger there, filling the reflective glass, then spreading beyond its borders. He noticed it almost a mile back when there were three other vehicles between it and him but still isn't sure he's being tailed. There's no reason he should be. The previous owner of the car he's driving wouldn't have called the police.

He's a dead man.

Then again, he doesn't yet know he's dead. His death is only now about to catch up with him, as it catches up with everyone eventually.

Not that the man would call the police in any case; for some folks police are the enemy, the mere presence of a blue uniform makes them twitchy, and this car's previous owner has been on the wrong side of the law for years.

So he and the police are hardly on friendly terms.

And anyway, can you really steal from a corpse? So this

one is a walking corpse. He'll be stilled soon enough, silenced soon enough. And wherever it is the dead go, they go naked, taking nothing with them. Even love they leave behind. And maybe that's wise. Possessions – and relationships – can be a burden. They bring responsibility with them, and responsibility is always heavy, even when accepted with grace. You feel it pressing down on you even when you don't realize it, like the weight of the atmosphere.

He's about to do this man a favor. He's about to lighten his load.

He sets fire to a cigarette and blows a stream of smoke out his open window.

The police car rolls by. The uniformed cop behind the wheel glances toward him, nods.

He touches the edge of his fedora with a leather-gloved hand, realizing too late that the cop might think it strange that his hands are covered in late May. But there's no double-take – the cop doesn't seem to register the glove at all, nor the recently broken nose, bent and swollen and pink with wiped-away blood, nor the gashed side of his head matted with the same – there's no reaction at all, the vehicle simply rolls by, so he steps into the bright suburban morning, sweating beneath his brown suit, the cotton fabric of his underclothes sticking to his skin.

A chain of nearly identical houses stretches along the street beneath a white Dallas sun like a hole punched in the blue to let the light in. Lawns that look as if the green's been applied with a brush. Porch swings creaking in the breeze. Fading hopscotch squares chalked across the sidewalk. Welcome mats that mean it.

The perfect hiding place for a career criminal. No one would ever suspect.

He glances right, watches the police car disappear around a corner, goodbye trouble, then walks to the trunk and keys it open. He flicks his cigarette to the street. Inside the trunk, a two-gallon gas can. He picks it up.

Gasoline sloshes within the can, which is about half full.

He crosses the now-empty street, walking toward one of the houses. Then up three concrete steps. He stops before a blue-painted front door. He grabs the doorknob and turns it. It unlatches. But it wouldn't have mattered if it hadn't; he has a set of keys – though he did leave them in the car. He pulls a large revolver from his waistband and steps lightly into the tiled foyer, looking around, cautious, gun at the ready. But it's quiet inside, peaceful. He closes his eyes and absorbs the quiet, lets it fill him. He projects a word in large white letters onto the interior wall of his otherwise dark skull: SILENCE.

Then to his left, at the other end of a long hallway, a sound.

He rubs his gloved thumb back and forth across the revolver's hammer spur, then heads in the direction from which the noise came.

The carpeted floor is nearly silent beneath his feet, merely whispering softly as the heels of his alligator-skin boots drag across the nap.

A closed door to his left. He pushes it open. Empty but for

furniture: two wing-back chairs and a coffee table in the middle of a book-lined room, a finger-printed scotch glass resting empty on the table beside a bottle of Glenfiddich.

An open door to his right revealing a bathroom, the corners dark with shadows.

His own reflection in the mirror above the sink startles him for a moment, but he recognizes himself almost instantly, so his gun hand barely twitches.

He continues to the end of the hallway, where a third door stands open.

I choose door number three.

Okay, sir, let's see what you win!

More noise issues from the room on the other side – drawers opening and closing, a baby crying, frantic conversation about hurry it up, we don't have much time.

A true fact: they have no time at all.

He steps into the doorway.

A man and woman hurriedly pack a suitcase which is laid out across a large unmade bed. Beside the suitcase lies a black briefcase. In a crib in the corner a baby sits red-eyed, snot running from its nose, its little fists clenched tight in fury.

He simply stands there, waiting to be noticed.

Soon enough he is. The man looks up, sees him, moves for a gun on a night table to his right – an automatic pistol – but the man's hand doesn't come within a foot of it.

Because he quickly raises his own gun, his revolver, thumbs back the hammer, and squeezes the trigger.

The man's head kicks hard to the right, like he was

whacked with an invisible baseball bat – home run, mother-fucker – and blood trickles down from within the hairline behind the temple, along his cheek at the front of his sideburn, and drips onto the left shoulder of a white shirt.

The man collapses.

The woman begins to scream.

He shoots her next, sending a piece of lead through her forehead at about a thousand feet per second. Her head kicks back hard, as if she were a PEZ dispenser – have some candy, kid – and the screaming stops.

He tosses the revolver to the floor, its purpose served, and walks to the bed. He opens the briefcase and looks inside, smiling at what he finds there. He latches the briefcase once more and lifts it, then begins dousing the place with gasoline, the fumes from the liquid making his eyes water. The smell is strong and hot in his nostrils.

The baby continues to wail as he pours gasoline onto the carpet.

He ignores it, tries to ignore it, and backs his way toward the front door, emptying the can – the last of the liquid swimming with flakes of rust – and after he's done he tosses it aside. It hits the floor and rings out hollow, like a cracked bell. He lights a match and watches it burn. The flame turns the blond wood black. He drops it to the floor before the flame reaches his nicotine-stained fingertips. The gasoline ignites with a whoosh, lighting up the place.

He steps back out into the sun with the briefcase in hand,

the sound of the baby's cries echoing in his skull, and makes his way across the street to the Chevy Impala.

Behind him, the house continues to burn.

He tries to shove aside thoughts of the screaming baby within, an innocent too young to be a problem, but he can hear its cries even now echoing within his skull.

He tries not to look over his shoulder. But of course he does look.

For a moment he watches orange flames flicker behind the glass of the bedroom window, as if it were a giant jack-o-lantern, then he once more walks toward the house. He feels very strongly that he will regret this decision, but he can't stop himself. Despite what he is there's something soft inside him, something that cannot tolerate the innocent wails of a child too young to speak.

Especially since he believes the child is his own.

NOW:

1

Andrew stepped into the warm air of the fading day and pulled the front door closed behind him. He could still hear the muffled sound of Melissa's angry voice coming from inside, but he ignored her curses and walked down the concrete steps to the parking lot which sat behind their apartment building. By the time he reached his car, a twenty-two-year-old MGB GT which had rolled off the lot the same year Nixon was elected to his first term, she'd been silenced by the distance between them. He fell in behind the steering wheel, turned the key in the ignition, pumped the gas pedal. The engine roared to life.

He sat motionless, both hands gripping the steering wheel. He stared through the windshield at nothing in particular. He exhaled.

A mere two weeks ago he'd have thought this

impossible. Now it was happening, it was reality, and all because of an old man's heart attack and a stack of envelopes left in a dresser drawer. He almost wished he hadn't found it – his life and his emotional state had been in turmoil since he innocently picked up that rubber-banded bundle – but he had, and the envelopes' contents could not be ignored. Not by him. There were too many questions that he needed answered. Questions he'd been asking for years.

He backed his car out of the parking spot and pulled out into the street. He listened to the radio while he drove and thought about nothing at all, and when he got where he was going fifteen minutes later he remembered not even so much as a single moment from the drive over. Had he stopped at red lights? He didn't know. Had he liked the songs that played on the radio? He couldn't even remember what they had been. Where the drive should have been in his memory was emptiness, a dark gap.

But this was nothing new: his entire history was a shelf of empty books. Take one out and flip through it, you'd only find blank pages one after the other forward to the end.

He pulled to the curb and killed the engine. He looked through the passenger window to the dilapidated facade of the Thirsty Fish. Someone who didn't know better might assume the place had gone bust several years ago – the windows painted black, the door closed, the neon sign unlighted – but he did know better, so he stepped with dirty Converse into the street, hopped up onto the gum-dotted sidewalk, made his way inside.

Any other bar he'd have been carded as soon as he pushed through the door – if you passed him on the street you'd see a skinny kid of maybe sixteen or seventeen in tattered Levi's and a T-shirt, with a bird's nest of choppy Supercuts-trimmed blond hair, sharp blue eyes, and acne scars still pink on his cheeks – but they knew him here, which meant they knew he wasn't exactly what he appeared to be. Skinny he was, five seven and a hundred and twenty pounds, but also a full decade older than he looked.

He stood in the doorway squinting at the other patrons as his eyes adjusted to the light in the room, or the lack thereof, darker by far than the early evening side-walk out front, and the faces came into focus, rose out of the darkness like surfacing sea creatures pale and round, but not one of them the face he wanted to see.

He glanced at his calculator watch and saw he was about ten minutes early. He ordered a beer and walked to an empty table in the corner. The table's surface was streaked and damp and had the musty stink of a days-in-use bar towel. He took a sip of his beer and set it down, wiped the moisture off his lip with the palm of his hand, then wiped the palm of his hand on his Levi's. He watched the door and felt sick to his stomach.

It wasn't every day you had the chance to track down the man who'd killed your mother.

And in his case that man was also his father.

He'd been in the room when it happened, but had also been a mere eighteen months old, far too young for memories to form – except he thought he *could* remember it. But maybe he was fooling himself. He knew he had at least one false memory, and it was as clear in his mind as the room which now surrounded him. Time had neither decayed nor rusted it.

A seven-year-old boy opens his eyes to find himself floating several feet above his bed, sheets and blankets hanging off him, as if off a high tree branch. He pushes them from his body and lets gravity take them. They fall in a pile to the mattress below. The ceiling is very close, only a foot or so from his face. He can see the texture so clearly, the fine cracks in the plaster. He pushes off the surface and swims through the air, pushes his way out of his bedroom, floats down the hallway. The air is cool and crisp and dark, but not so dark that he can't see. He can see everything as he floats into the dining room, over the dining table and the bowl of fruit which rests there. Everything is sharp with color, vibrant. If he wanted to, he could reach down and pluck an apple from the bowl, but he doesn't want to. Instead, he pushes himself off the walls in the room, and laughs as he bounces from one to another, moving effortlessly and with grace. He feels wonderful and free and full of joy.

It was, in fact, the only time he could remember feeling that way – absolutely without burden – but the memory wasn't real and couldn't be, for it was filled with impossibilities. He knew it wasn't real despite the persistent feeling that it absolutely *had* to be. It had to be because it felt like a memory – not a dream, not a fantasy, but a memory – and people did not remember things that hadn't happened.

Except apparently they did.

So maybe what he remembered of his mother's murder was false as well. Maybe his memory was only of his visualization of descriptions in newspaper articles he'd read years later while huddled before a microfilm reader in the public library.

Even if the event had been so traumatic as to burn itself into his brain, as to brand itself upon his brain, there was no reason to believe his recollection was accurate. He'd heard once while listening to public radio that every time you remembered an event you were only recalling your last recollection, not the memory itself. The person who'd explained this, a scientist discussing his research, had compared the mind to an old VHS tape. Each time you remembered something, he'd said, you were in effect making a new recording of the event, taping over your last memory even as you recalled it, and with each new recording the quality was poorer. New errors entered the memory, false information. Your current state of mind affected how you perceived it and could even change events. Blue cars became green cars. Grass became asphalt. Good weather became poor.

So it was possible that his recollection of his mother's murder was false, but he didn't think so. He knew his memory of flying was not genuine because it was filled with impossible things – and because it *was* so clear. None of his actual memories from his childhood were nearly so vivid. They were each nothing but a length of grainy footage full of scratches and unlighted corners. His memory of his mother's murder was the same.

Which made him believe it was real.

He took another swallow of his beer and stared at the wall, onto which he saw projected his own past, his first and oldest memory.

He sits in a wooden crib wearing nothing but a cloth diaper. One of the safety pins has come unsnapped and is digging into his leg. He cries for his mother, wants her to make it feel better, wants her to pick him up and hold him. But she does none of those things. Instead, she hurriedly packs a suitcase. A man who isn't Daddy helps her. He says something to her, but Andrew doesn't understand most of his words. All he understands is that something is wrong. This man feels panicked and his mother feels panicked as well. He can sense that much even without understanding what they're saying. Then Daddy steps into the doorway. He stands there for a long time – and why won't Mommy pick him up? He cries and cries, but she won't pick him up. Then Daddy raises his arm and in his hand is a strange metal thing, large and black. There's a loud bang. The thing in Daddy's hand makes the sound, and Daddy's hand kicks back. The man who isn't Daddy falls to the ground. Mommy screams. She screams loudly. Maybe the bang scared her, he doesn't know, but it scared him, and her scream-

ing scares him too, crazy and out of control, and it makes him cry even louder. Then there's another bang and Mommy stops screaming. She falls to the ground. Daddy pours something onto the carpet. It smells bad and it makes it hard to breathe. He can feel the fumes from it in the back of his nose. His eyes water. Daddy backs out of the room. Several moments later the flames come. They come rushing in on the carpet. They come rushing in through the door. They burn hot and terrible all around him. He's never felt such heat, never been so scared. Why doesn't Mommy get up? Why doesn't she get up and come to him? Why doesn't she pick him up and take him away from here? She shouldn't be sleeping now. He cries for her, cries loudly, shaking his tiny fists, but she doesn't move. Then Daddy returns. He walks through the flames and the smoke and picks him up. He carries him through the flames, through black smoke and the stink of things burning that were never meant to burn. He carries him through the front door and into daylight bright and hot and clean. The sky is very blue. A summer breeze blows warm against his skin.

That was where the memory ended – the one memory his father had left him with – with the bright sun shining down on him. Then the screen of his mind went black and did not light up again until he was three, maybe four, and living with his grandparents, his mother dead, his father missing and probably dead as well.

He was glad the man had come back for him, it meant he'd not been completely heartless despite what he'd done, but he couldn't forgive him. Neither for that nor for what he'd left behind: a son who made people think of a cold-blooded killer. It was in the way he walked, his love of history, the way he closed his eyes when angry; it was even in the rhythm and tone of his speech: people who'd known the man – Andrew's grandparents, his uncle Burt – said he was very much his father's son. It made him feel responsible for a murder he'd had no part in, and it made him hate himself a little bit. For wasn't he a replica of this man he despised?

He wanted to find his father, to face him. He didn't know why, didn't know what he might get out of it, didn't know what he would do once he was face-to-face with the man, but he knew it was something he needed to do. Yet for years it seemed impossible. The man had vanished. There was a public record – in 1955 his father had been charged with and found not guilty of conspiracy to commit murder; in 1957 he'd gone to prison for assaulting a police officer; between 1960 and 1963 there were several newspaper articles mentioning that he had ties to organized crime in the southwest and was suspected of being involved in various homicides – but after the day his mother was killed, twenty-six years ago now, Harry Combs had ceased to exist, had simply vanished off the face of the earth, air filling in the space he'd once displaced.

Maybe he was rotting in an unmarked grave somewhere. He'd certainly lived that kind of life. But Andrew wanted to know with certainty, and that didn't seem possible.

But as he made a life for himself he thought of his father less. He spent three years majoring in American History at California State University, Long Beach, then dropped out and got work in construction, which he liked far more than he'd expected he would. There was a sense of pride he got from it that he didn't get from intellectual pursuits. He felt like he'd actually *done* something when he drove by a house he'd helped to build: there was the proof, taking up space in the world. He met a girl named Melissa and they moved in together. He bought a fifty-dollar ring from K-Mart and proposed. She said yes and despite their use of birth control almost immediately got pregnant. But they weren't ready for that – together they barely made enough money to cover the bills; if she had to quit her job to take care of a child they'd go under – so after hours of late-night discussions she'd had an abortion. It was difficult, and she'd cried about it afterwards (she wanted a child yet knew better than to have one now), but it hadn't hurt their relationship. They continued to live together and love each other, and they continued their engagement without worrying about *when* they might actually get married.

His life wasn't the one he'd imagined as a child, it was none of the lives he'd imagined as a child, but it was a good life nonetheless, a life he felt comfortable in.

Then last week his grandfather had a heart attack and everything changed.

He'd grown up in Buena Park, California, with his

paternal grandparents looking after him. He didn't know the story of how he ended up there – neither of them talked much, particularly when it came to painful matters (when he was ten, rather than tell him a cousin had died in a car accident, they told him to put on his church suit and simply drove him to the funeral) – but they were the only close family he had, his mother's parents being dead, so when his grandmother called him from the hospital and told him what had happened and asked him to go to their house and pack some clothes and other items into a duffel bag, he'd said of course, grandma, and headed out the door immediately.

His grandfather died while he was packing the duffel bag, but he didn't find that out until his arrival at the hospital later, at which point he went into the nearest bathroom, punched the walls, tore the paper towel dispenser down, stared at himself in the mirror and cried. He thought about the only man in his life being dead, thought about the man who had raised him being dead, and he thought about what he had found in the man's dresser which proved, finally, that his father, whom he'd suspected dead for years, was in fact alive.

For it was while he was loading up that duffel bag that he found the bundle of envelopes. It was tucked into one of the dresser drawers, hidden behind several pairs of rolled socks.

Without thinking about what he was doing he pulled the rubber band away and examined the envelopes. None of them bore a return address but each was postmarked either Clarksville or New Albany, Indiana. There were twenty-five in all. The earliest was from 1964, the most recent from last year. He opened the earliest and pulled from within a time-yellowed typewritten letter.

Dear Mom and Dad,

I hope you're both well. Andy's second birthday is right around the corner. Thinking about it makes me miss him. I wish I could see his face, but we all know that isn't possible. I'm sending some money for you to buy him a birthday present, and to buy baby food and other necessities as well. Whatever you need. I hope it's enough. I know expenses add up.

H

He rubbed his thumb across the handwritten 'H' at the bottom of the letter, feeling the grooves in the paper left by his father's pen, for it was his father who had sent this letter and all the others, and as he did he wondered what the man was doing in that same moment. Was he sitting on a couch somewhere watching television? Was he grocery shopping? Was he pressing the barrel of a gun against the back of someone's head?

This was the closest he'd ever gotten to him, the only

indication he'd ever had that the man was still alive, but if his grandfather had not died on the same day he found the letters he might have been able to leave it alone. Probably not – but maybe.

Either way, it was only later, in the hospital bathroom, while thinking of his dead grandfather, his knuckles bloody and bruised, that he knew he was going to track his father down. Something within him demanded they meet.

He wanted to look this man in the eyes and – and what? He didn't know. He simply felt it would offer some kind of understanding.

For his grandfather was dead and could offer none himself. Not that he would have had he been alive. Everything the man had said to him in the twenty-six years Andrew had known him could easily fit on one side of a Post-it note.

What he knew from his grandfather was what he could learn from the man's behavior, and what he learned was that while the man might love him there was hatred there as well. His quiet grandfather hated him for walking like Harry Combs, for talking like him, for having a temper like him and a capacity for violence.

Andrew's grandfather hated him for the same reasons Andrew hated himself.

Andrew had to confront his father. He *had* to.

It was something he needed to do in order that he might shed his father's skin and become himself.

And wasn't that what it meant to be a man?

He hired a private detective to help find him – he didn't know where to begin himself but knew a man could not spend a quarter century anywhere without leaving evidence of himself behind – and earlier today that detective had phoned him saying they should meet.

That could mean only one thing.

He told Melissa what he was doing as he was getting ready to leave, and she told him he was an idiot, told him that stirring up the mud of his past could never offer clarity, told him she loved him and didn't want to see him get hurt, told him he should stop this before it went any further. He told her mind your own fucking business and it became a fight. They were a couple and had been for some time, which meant his business *was* her business. If he didn't understand that, maybe they should call off the whole thing. He said maybe we should, you meddlesome cunt, though he didn't mean it, and after watching her wither and feeling a coldness wash over him stepped out into the fading daylight, pulling the front door closed behind him. He walked down the concrete steps that led to the parking lot and got into his car. He drove to a dive bar about fifteen minutes from his Long Beach apartment, and he now sat at a table there, drinking a beer and watching the door.

She didn't understand. She came from a family which was whole. She had a mother and a father and two older brothers. They ate together during the holidays and laughed. They talked on the phone. There was no absence in her life like a missing tooth the tongue kept going to. That wasn't her fault, of course, but the fact remained: she didn't understand emptiness; she didn't understand the aching hollow of absence.

The door swung open and a heavy-set man in a white linen suit squeezed his way into the bar, pulling off a straw fedora and fanning his sweating red face with it. In his other hand he held a manila envelope and a purple folder. There was no mistaking him. It was Francis Martin, the private detective Andrew had hired.

Andrew raised a hand and after a moment Martin spotted him, nodded, and shuffled over, breathing heavily from the twenty steps it took to get from the door to the table. Andrew noticed for the first time that despite the suit the man was wearing sneakers, and slits had been cut into them to give his feet room. The socked flesh squeezed through the slits like bread dough.

'Mr Combs,' he said, settling into one of the wooden chairs, its legs creaking under his weight. He started to put his hat onto the table, but hesitated, seeming not to like the look of the dirty surface, and after a moment decided simply to set it back on his head.

'Did you want something to drink?'

'No, thank you. Gluttony is my vice.'

Andrew nodded. 'Did you find him?'

'First, the matter of money.'

Andrew stiffened. 'I paid you.'

'You paid something, yes, but it didn't quite cover my expenses despite my working very hard to do the job within those financial confines. There were long-distance telephone calls, fuel charges, and I had to coordinate with a southern private detective who cost a hundred and fifty dollars a day for his two days of work. It adds up, you see, and in the end that other fellow is still making more money than I am, though you employed me to handle this affair.'

'What do you claim I owe you?'

'It isn't much.'

He opened the purple folder, removed a sheet of paper, and attempted to slide it across the table. But the moisture on the table's surface put a stop to any movement.

Andrew reached out and picked it up, glanced down at it, read the itemized expenses less the five hundred dollars he'd already paid the man, and saw that, according to the invoice, he owed another forty-three.

He relaxed some. 'I have forty on me.'

Martin nodded. 'That will suffice.'

Andrew leaned left, pulled his canvas wallet from his right hip pocket, peeled back the Velcro, slid out two twenties, set them on the table.

Martin plucked them up gingerly, folded them in half, slid them into his pocket.

'Very well.'

He handed Andrew the manila envelope.

Andrew straightened the bent metal clasp and unfolded

the top. He pulled out two photographs and a short type-written report. His father looked old and tired in the pictures, which surprised him. His hair was brittle and gray, his face lined with wrinkles. He had spent so many hours looking at a single photograph from 1962 – a photograph in which his father stood grinning with his arm wrapped around Andrew's very pregnant mother – that he'd expected to see the young man his father had been rather than the old one he'd become. For some reason it hadn't occurred to him that though he'd vanished his father had continued to live and breathe and age in the real world. It didn't seem right somehow.

This was somebody he barely recognized.

He set the pictures down and looked over the report. His father, who had changed his last name to White, lived not in Clarksville or New Albany, Indiana, but in Louis-ville, Kentucky. He'd married a local woman in 1968 and the marriage continued. He ran a new-and-used bookshop on Bardstown Road and lived in a brick Cape Cod in the Highlands. He was a respectable and respected middle-class gentleman whom everyone knew and liked.

Andrew stared down at the report silently for some time before looking up.

'I guess we're done here,' he said.

He put the photographs and the report back into the manila envelope in which they'd been delivered, fastened the clasp, got to his feet. He walked to the door and through it. If asked he wouldn't have been able to describe his emotional state; it was simply a strange, slightly confused numbness. But despite this he knew what he was next going to do. He supposed it had never been in question.

He unlocked his car and slipped in behind the wheel.

The morning light splashed in through the window bright and hot. Normally he didn't like that the bedroom window caught the sunrise, it made sleeping in impossible, and when he had a day off he didn't like to be up before noon, but, despite it being Sunday, he was up and showered by six o'clock this morning, and had waited that long only because he wanted to put off his inevitable fight with Melissa for as long as possible. Most of the night he'd lain awake, staring at the ceiling, waiting for sunlight to hit his window shade.

His turning mind would not allow sleep. He wanted to get on the road.

He leaned down and pulled his suitcase out from under the bed. He'd bought it for a trip to San Francisco four years ago and hadn't used it since. He set it on the mattress and opened it, discovering a pair of underwear he'd long thought lost and a tube of toothpaste. He wondered if toothpaste went bad, but didn't think so, and when he searched for an expiration date failed to find one, though he didn't look hard and could have missed it. It didn't matter. He tucked it into one of the inside pockets, and went about packing, aware of but trying to ignore Melissa as she stood in the doorway with her arms crossed, glaring at him with both tight-lipped fury and something like fear.

'I can't believe you're doing this.'

'I don't think I'll be gone long. I just have to see him.'

'Why?'

He looked up at her, opened his mouth to speak, but had nothing to say. The *why* was a feeling in the pit of his stomach, something like dread but not dread, and he couldn't tell her that. It wouldn't mean anything. He knew she deserved an answer – he *owed* her an answer – but he had no answer to give her. So he merely stood silent and looked across the room at her. She was beautiful. Even angry she was beautiful. Maybe more beautiful for her anger. It put a fire into her eyes. He thought briefly of asking her to come with him but knew that could never work. What he had to do he had to do alone.

This was *his* thing, whatever it was, and she'd only get in the way. She'd only spend their time together trying to talk him into turning his car around.

'I'm sorry,' he said.

She shook her head. 'I don't care about that. I care about *you*. Can't you see you're making a mistake? This can't end well. Just – just leave it alone, Andy.'

She didn't understand emptiness like a missing tooth the tongue could not leave be.

'I can't,' he said. 'If I could I would, but I can't.'

He finished packing. When he was done he closed the suitcase and latched it. He hefted it off the mattress and carried it toward the bedroom door. He stopped and looked at Melissa. She looked back.

'I'm leaving,' he said.

She nodded, but said nothing.

He kissed the corner of her mouth – she did not kiss him back – and then walked past her to the front door, once more feeling a coldness wash over him. She could burst into flames in this moment and he would feel nothing.

He pulled it open and stepped into the cool morning sunlight.

He had a long drive ahead of him.

2

Teresa was already sitting at the kitchen table when Harry walked into the room at seven forty-five. He was showered and dressed, wearing slacks, a shirt and tie, and an old cardigan with holes in the shoulders from too many years on a hanger. She had put on a bathrobe in her stumble from bed to kitchen and slouched now with a glass and a bottle of vodka at her side. The bottle was filmed with ice from a night in the freezer, and the glass was for the moment empty. But Teresa's eyes were glossy and the empty glass was wet with condensation, both of which meant she'd already consumed at least a double – she had to start immediately or she began to shake uncontrollably – and she was certain to consume more. In fact, the large bottle, half full at the moment, would almost certainly be empty by the time he returned home from the bookshop this evening. That was just the way it went.

He walked over to her and kissed her temple.

'Morning.'

'You look handsome.' She smiled crookedly.

'Want some breakfast before I head out?'

She shrugged.

He nodded and walked to the refrigerator. 'I'll fix you some breakfast.'

If he didn't she was likely to go the entire day without eating anything. She was likely to puke up most of what he gave her anyway, but she'd digest at least some of it before she reached that point, and he felt the need to do what he could.

After scanning the shelves for a moment, he pulled out four eggs, a package of bacon, and a bag of spinach. He chopped up four slices of bacon and threw them into a skillet, then put the eggs into a small saucepan and covered them with water. While the eggs came to a boil and the bacon cooked he made himself a cup of instant coffee and sipped it, staring out the kitchen window to his backyard.

He had a small raised garden out back in which he grew herbs and vegetables, and since it was the height of summer now, it was wild with color. He hadn't planned on a raised bed, but when he was shoveling out sod in the early winter of 1967, the year he bought the house, he'd hit a slab of concrete which had turned out to be a septic-tank cover from before the city's plumbing system had made it out to this part of Louisville. Since he couldn't go down he went up, built a cedar garden box from fence planks and brought in a mixture of topsoil and composted manure and humus to fill it.

In addition to the septic tank he'd come across a small toy soldier: a little green man with a little green gun. He'd accidentally cut off its legs with his shovel while removing the sod, but found them, cleaned up both parts of the toy, rinsed them of dirt, and glued the pieces back together. He set the toy soldier on a shelf in his library upstairs where it stood guard even now, somewhat dustier than when he'd first set it down but in the same condition otherwise. His son would have been five years old back when he found it – would have turned five only a couple weeks earlier – and probably played with just such things. He could imagine him sitting on a carpeted floor in the midst of his toy soldiers, playing war, saying, 'Oh no, they shot me – shot me *dead*,' playing out scenes he'd watched in movies or on TV, the real world far away.

That was a small part why he maintained the garden even now: it was where he'd found that stupid toy soldier. But the real reason was his first wife. Helen had always talked about starting a vegetable garden, eating what they grew. She was excited by the prospect of food going straight from their garden to their mouths; but she was killed before she got the chance to turn her thoughts into reality – killed by *him* – and since she could no longer do it, he did it for her. As if it could somehow erase what he'd done. As if it could fill the hole left inside him.

And in some small way he felt that he was putting in his time.

The fact was that he did it because, for reasons he didn't fully understand, he *had* to do it.

As he had to stay in his second marriage despite what Teresa had become. He'd killed his first wife and lost his son; *this* relationship he would make work. He owed it not only to Teresa but to Helen, who had died for his sins.

But he also stayed because he loved Teresa. She drank too much, was killing herself with alcohol, but she had her reasons, which he knew all too well, and those reasons were probably why they had ended up together in the first place. They'd understood one another on a gut level without need for words. He couldn't leave her for the very reason he loved her. What kind of man would do such a thing?

Perhaps the man he'd once been, but not the man he now was.

He plucked each piece of bacon from the skillet one after the other with a pair of tongs and set them on a paper towel, then dropped great handfuls of spinach into the rendered bacon fat. He added salt, pepper and a clove of garlic, chopped, and once the spinach had cooked down he added the bacon back into the skillet and a small dollop of heavy cream. He scooped the spinach onto plates and peeled the eggs. He cut the eggs in half and set them on the beds of spinach, watching as runny yolk leaked across their plates. Then he set a plate in front of Teresa and ate his own breakfast standing up at the counter.

When he was done he rinsed his plate and his cup and set them in the sink.

'Don't worry about the dishes,' he said. 'I'll get to them after work.'

He kissed the corner of her mouth – smelling alcohol on her breath sour and hot – and headed out the front door.

He parked behind the building and let himself in through a rusty green-painted back door, which he then propped open with a brick so customers who used the parking lot didn't have to walk around to the front to get inside; often they were carrying bags or boxes loaded with books. He turned on the lights and checked that Tom Selleck had plenty of food and water in his bowls. The mustachioed orange tabby looked up from his small bed on the floor, meowed once, good morning, and lazily closed his eyes again. Harry scratched him behind the left ear a moment before making his way to the front of the store.

Three cardboard boxes full of paperbacks and several

stacks of hardbacks he'd accepted for store credit sat on the counter, and he knew he needed to inventory and shelve them – he had a bad habit of letting books pile up around the store, and often had no idea where anything was when customers asked for specific items, though he was certain he had them – but he had all day to get to it – hell, the pile was small enough that he could put it off till tomorrow or the day after; stock had been much further backlogged before – and didn't feel any great urge to alphabetize this early in the morning, nor to consider what section certain books ought to be placed in, so he simply sat in his chair and looked out through the picture window to the moderate flow of traffic on Bardstown Road. The store didn't open for another twenty minutes and he planned to do nothing but sit here until then.

Maybe he'd hire someone part time to organize the store for him. He could drive down to the University of Louisville after he closed up tonight and tack up a few notices. He was sure to get applicants, and since they'd be college students most of them would know how to read.

Or maybe he'd just tape something up in his front door. That seemed easier.

A knock on the window.

A bearded man in an open-necked silk shirt and a white summer coat waved at him with gold-ringed fingers, then took a drag from a cigarillo.

Harry shook his head and tapped his watch, which was usually enough to make people understand the place wasn't open yet and he had no intention of opening early, but this guy only shook his head back at him, then nodded in the direction of the front door.

Harry sighed, pushed himself to his feet, and shuffled over to the finger-printed glass door, which he unlocked and pulled open.

'We're closed,' he said. 'That's why the sign says "closed". If you can read a book, you can read a goddamn sign. Come back in twenty minutes if I haven't been too rude.'

He started to push the door shut, but paused when the man said, 'I'm not here about no books, Mr Combs.'

At the sound of his old name – absent from his life for so many years – his stomach went sour and a lead ball dropped into his gut, splashing bitterness into his throat. He swallowed. 'I'm afraid you have me mistaken for some-one else.'

The man shook his head. 'I don't think so, no. You're you.'

'I don't have time for this.'

He tried to push the door shut but before it could latch the man stopped its arc with a leather-shoed foot size twelve.

'I think you wanna make time, yeah?'

'No.'

Harry stomped on the man's foot with the heel of his own and when the man cursed and pulled back he shoved the door shut and latched it.

'If you want to talk,' he said through the glass, 'come back in twenty minutes when we're open. I don't make time.'

He returned to his chair and sat down.

After twenty-six years his past had finally caught up with him. He didn't know why or how, but that it had was indisputable – like a boomerang which had finally come back around to whack him in the head. It made him feel sick. He was too old to go on the run again. He was too old to start a new life. And he couldn't abandon Teresa, anyway. She wouldn't make it alone, and he wouldn't make it on the run with her slowing him down. So this was it. This was what he had. He kept it or he lost it, but this was all there was for him.

Even if he had a chance on the run he didn't think he'd take it. He didn't think he could handle it. He'd lost his first life in a blaze – lost his wife and his son – and he didn't think he could handle losing this life too, not after he'd spent so many years living in it.

After a while the box you're in becomes your world, what exists outside it ceases to matter, and when that box is destroyed you'd rather be destroyed with it than try to step out into the universe beyond.

Perhaps that was why captains went down with their ships. The universe beyond was less welcoming than death. For at least in death there was peace rather than that strange sense of being lost – completely lost, in self and in life.

He hoped there was peace in death, anyway. What a cruel and sick joke it would be to die and wake up elsewhere.

Even heaven would be hell if it lasted for eternity.

He looked out the window and watched the man walk across the street to his car, a black Honda Prelude – figured the son of a bitch wouldn't buy American – and slide into the vehicle. After a moment, the man lit a new cigarillo from the butt of his old one, cracked his window, flicked the butt into the street, and blew a stream of smoke into the air while looking toward Harry. His face was expressionless, dead as stone.

Without any further information Harry already knew two things about the guy: he did not have ties to anyone in Dallas and he was not a cop. These were facts. If he'd come here from Texas Harry would already be dead, and if he were a cop Harry would already have been arrested, and not by a lone man with gold rings on his fingers and breath like the stale beer in cans littered around a house the morning after a party. But even with those possibilities eliminated he didn't feel much closer to discovering who the man actually *was*, and that was something he needed to know before he decided how to proceed.

Of course, he also needed to know what the man wanted. He could have learned that already if he'd let him into the store, but there was never any chance of that happening. You let someone get away with pushing you once they'll take it for granted you *can* be pushed. No, he'd wait the twenty minutes. It was a small thing but important.

In the meantime he needed to look unconcerned. He picked up an old Lion paperback, a worn copy of Jim Thompson's *A Hell of a Woman*, and pretended to read about Frank Dillon's downfall. But of course he was incapable of focusing long enough to read and comprehend even so much as a single sentence. His mind kept turning to this man outside his store.

Twenty-six years he had gone without being uncovered. He lived a normal life in a town where no one knew what he'd once been. Most of the people walking the streets didn't even remember a time when he wasn't here. Like an old building he was ever present and therefore taken for granted. Something stays around long enough you stop seeing it. It's only the unfamiliar you notice – the new mustache, the new pair of glasses.

But something had happened to change that. Something had brought him to someone's attention, something outside himself. He didn't know what or who, but he knew he didn't like it.

He didn't like it at all.

He was supposed to be an old shoe, always present in the closet but never worn, never even seen. He was supposed to be a dilapidated shotgun house in Germantown rotting away in anonymity while people walked by every day unnoticing.

He was supposed to be invisible.

*

At nine o'clock he unlocked the front door, flipped the sign, turned around, and walked back to the chair behind the counter. He sat down, chair creaking under his weight.

Less than a minute later the man in the silk shirt pushed his way into the place. He had a cocky strut that made Harry want to knock him down. That might eliminate some of the arrogance evidenced in his posture and his face. A little violence went a long way toward knocking away a man's facade and revealing the interior rooms of the heart. Arrogance didn't matter then – nor did money, upbringing, or education.

All men were equal when they had guns to their heads.

'You're not a cop and you're not here from Dallas, so what do you want?'

'I used to be a cop. Little further south than Louisville, though.'

'I didn't ask for your résumé, I asked what you wanted.'

The man laughed. 'Fair enough.' His face went suddenly cold, revealing no trace of the humor which had a moment earlier lighted it. 'Ten grand.'

Harry was silent almost a full minute. Then: 'I run a bookstore. Occasionally I'll sell a new hardcover and bring in a whopping ten or twelve bucks in profit, before overhead, but I deal mostly in used paperbacks. Charge half of cover price when I can get it, which is generally three bucks or so in case you haven't picked up a book lately, and from the look of you you haven't, and that's after I put out a buck to buy it, so two dollars in profit if I'm lucky, again before overhead, but almost thirty percent of my regulars deal primarily in store credit. In other words, a lot of business consists of nothing but trading books for more books. So where on earth do you think I'm gonna get ten thousand dollars, and what makes you think I would simply hand it to you even if I managed to get my hands on that kind of money?'

The man smiled. 'You don't need to get the ten thousand dollars because you already got it. I don't know where it is, but I know it exists. That much and more. But I'm not a greedy man. This little bookshop of yours isn't about money. It's about you looking like a regular Joe who does a regular thing for a living. So don't tell me about how little you make. I don't care. And you'll give me the ten grand because you like your life here, and you know damn well I can kick it out from under you. So let's cut the shit, do our business in as pleasant a manner as possible, and get on with our lives – yeah?'

Harry clenched his jaw and looked across the counter. The man looking back was calm, relaxed. It infuriated him. 'If I was the man I used to be you'd be dead already.'

'If you was the man you used to be *you'd* be dead already – you'd have been dead for a quarter century – and I can make you that man again.'

'How'd you find me?'

'It's what I do.'

'Private detective. Who *sent* you to find me?'

'I don't see how that has anything to do with our current situation.'

'If someone else knows who and where I am, paying you off doesn't do me any good.'

'The person who made the enquiry ain't gonna call the police.'

'You can't guarantee that.'

'Even if I can't you'd rather have the chance of safety than the certain knowledge of going down, wouldn't you?'

Harry closed his eyes a moment to think. He opened them.

'I don't have the money lying around. I live on what the bookshop brings in. You start a new life, it has to look authentic, which means it has to *be* authentic. I can get you the money, but it requires a drive up to Indianapolis, and I'm not going to make that drive today. You come back on Wednesday, I'll have it for you.'

The man shook his head. 'No – I want it today. Indianapolis ain't that far. It's what, a four-hour round trip? You leave now you can have the money by lunchtime.'

'I could, but I won't.'

'You don't seem to realize who's in charge of this situation.'

'You need to shut your damn fool mouth about being in charge. We both know you have to wait. You're not going to the cops. If you did you wouldn't get your money. You've got me – I know it and you know it – but let's not pretend you get to dictate to me how this goes down. You don't. You want the money you'll wait for it.'

The man was silent for a long time. Harry could see him thinking, trying to figure a way to get what he wanted. But finally he gave up. 'Okay,' he said. 'I guess I wait. I'll see you in a couple days, Mr Combs.'

'Don't call me that again,' Harry said. 'It's no longer who I am.'

The workday passed. He shelved books. He sold books. He bought a first-edition copy of *A Farewell to Arms* from a pawnbroker he knew – guy always came into the shop when something like that turned up – and put it in the glass case behind the counter beside a first edition of *As I Lay Dying*. It didn't have a dust jacket, so it wasn't worth as much as the guy had hoped, but it was still a first edition, and a first printing of that edition. When eight o'clock came around, he locked up, turned off the lights, scratched Tom Selleck behind the ear for a minute or so, and headed out into the evening.

It was still hot out despite the setting of the sun – July in Louisville could be hellish, and he tended to dress without regard for the weather, since he spent very little of his time out in it – and as soon as he stepped from the air-conditioned bookshop his clothes began sticking to him. He removed his old cardigan and rolled up his sleeves before sliding into his car.

He wanted to bury that goddamn private detective. He hadn't killed in twenty-six years, but he found that some of the coldness was still in him. It was buried deep, pushed down and down, but he had no doubt he could release it once more, let it begin to flow through his veins.

But he would not.

He was no longer Harry Combs, killer. He was Harry White, bookseller.

He had spent twenty-six years rebuilding himself as a new man, and that was who he was going to remain.

He had changed even before his name had. Losing Helen had changed him. Losing Helen had made him understand death in ways that two years as an army sniper, two years as a government operative, and fifteen years as a private sector contractor never had, in ways that even the death of his older sister when he was seventeen never had. Helen had been his constant companion for years. She was the person he woke up to every morning, the person with whom he ate his meals, the person with whom he shared his dreams, the person he fell asleep beside every night. Losing her – killing her – broke him, shattered the man he had been.

And when after years he finally healed, when he finally glued himself back together, he was shaped differently than he had been when she was still alive.

The places he had been broken were stronger now, but they still bore evidence of his self-inflicted tragedy.

He understood pain and loss in ways he never had

before, and that understanding carried with it an empathy which he'd never before possessed. He also carried with him the parts of her she'd given him, and since she'd been a better person than he, he became a better person for having shared his life with her.

They say you get over such a loss, but it isn't true. Even after you put yourself back together you ache in the places where you were broken. You simply learn to live with the pain. You come to accept that sometimes – even ten years later, or twenty – you will see something that reminds you of your loss – a glass like one she once drank out of, a willow tree like one you once picnicked under – and all of those places you should be healed will hurt again, and your heart will ache like a broken bone with rain impending.

No one who's not suffered such a loss can comprehend how it changes a person. They may think they can – they may think the loss of a parent or a sibling gives them some insight into what it means – but they're wrong. There is no pain of loss like that pain of loss.

And his pain was perhaps greater even than that of others who had suffered similar losses, for he was also its source.

Helen's death was not caused by disease or freak accident. It was not something that could be tossed at the feet of an unjust god or an entropic universe. He didn't even believe in God, though for months after Helen's death he tried very hard to believe. Faith would have been a great salve, for he wanted to see her again more than he wanted anything else.

And he wanted forgiveness.

But mostly he wanted not to be responsible for erasing her existence. If there were a heaven she might at least exist there, and if she existed there he hadn't killed her after all. He had simply helped her to the next plane. He had simply guided her home.

But he did not believe.

There was no heaven. There was no forgiveness. And there was no God at whose feet he could lay the blame.

He was the reason she was dead. He was the reason he could never hold her again. He was the reason her beautiful laughter was absent from the world.

And the world was colder for that loss.

He started his car.

When he got home he found Teresa lying on the kitchen floor in her own sick. The bottle on the table was empty. She moaned, God, I'm so sorry, and began to cry when he lifted her. Bits of vomit had dried to the front of her robe and her cheek and when he lifted her they fell away. He carried her into the bathroom and set her into the tub, then removed the robe and her shirt as well as her pajama bottoms. She looked thin and wasted, hip bones jutting, breasts like empty sacks. Her pubic hair was thick and unkempt, speckled with gray. She smelled sour and somehow fruity. He turned on the faucet, adjusted the water's temperature, then pulled the lever which started the shower.

After washing her and brushing her teeth – spit for me, sweetheart – he dried her off as well as he could, lifted her in his arms – upsy-daisy – and carried her into the bedroom. She opened her eyes and smiled at him as he put her into bed, her eyes glassy and far away.

'You're a good man, Harry White.'

'Get a little sleep,' he said, 'I'll wake you for dinner.'

'Okay.'

She closed her eyes. He turned and walked out into the hallway. He stopped in the bathroom to urinate, looked at himself in the mirror. When he was in his early thirties and the first gray hairs had begun appearing on his head he'd felt a strange sense of pride in them. He'd *earned* those gray hairs. Now there was nothing on his head *but* gray, and he didn't feel proud about it. He'd been a pretty crummy human being when he was younger – some would have called him evil, though he did not believe in such a thing – but he missed his youth.

Yes, but it was gone.

He went into the kitchen and cleaned up the floor. Then loaded the dishwasher, put a soap tablet into the machine, and got it running.

When he was done, he walked upstairs to his library. He sat in a leather chair and looked across the room to his safe. It wasn't much of a safe, just a black metal box with a dial on the front – a man with a crowbar and a weighty hammer could have opened it in no time flat – but it contained what he had kept of his old life.

After a few minutes he got to his feet and opened the safe. He looked inside. Twenty-two stacks of bills, each stack containing ten thousand dollars; a small automatic pistol; a Texas driver's license that had expired in 1965; a picture of Helen smiling and holding their infant son; a folded-up piece of blue fabric, the shirt Helen had worn on the night they met.

And that was it; that was everything.

He looked at the picture of Helen for a long time, then brought her shirt to his face and inhaled its scent. Her smell was no longer present on the fabric, it smelled only of dust, but it helped him to imagine that scent he had lost himself in on so many nights.

Part of him wished he could forget. Part of him wished he could simply erase that life from his memory.

But most of him wanted to keep the past alive.

He'd always despised people who harvested their pain, who tended to it year in and year out in order only to eat its bitter fruit – he found them to be so fucking *weak* – so it was strange to think that he might actually be one of them. But if the pain died, that would mean the love had died too, and that he could not stand.

For as much as he loved Teresa, and he did, the fact remained that if Helen were alive he would be with her even now – for better or for worse.

Unless he was fooling himself. It was possible that he had been for years. He knew that since her death he had created an idealized version of his first wife, and had spent his time remembering only the best parts of their relationship rather than the endless fights, the cheating, the threats of divorce. He knew those things existed but had pushed them to the back of his mind. It felt wrong to remember Helen that way, though those memories were as true as the good ones. It made him feel guilty, somehow, to think ill of the dead.

But maybe if he remembered her wholly, if he remembered and internalized everything she had been – everything their relationship had been – maybe then he'd actually be able to let her go. Why was he clinging to a dead love? Why was he allowing himself to sink with it? It made no sense, did it? You don't cling to a stone to keep afloat, and dead love is the heaviest stone there is. Loving someone who will not or cannot love you back is a form of suicide. Only love that is reciprocated is weightless.

If he could let it go, if he could give himself fully to Teresa, who was here now, maybe she would not drown herself in vodka. Maybe it was not the loss she had suffered which caused her drinking. Maybe it was her every day. Maybe it was the fact she had spent over twenty-two years with a man who had only given her half of himself. Maybe the fact that she was clinging to him while he sank was the reason she was drowning too.

And her drowning was far more literal, far more desperate.

And yet he could not release that dead love. He could not simply let it go and swim back to the surface.

He knew why. He knew it was guilt that made him do it, guilt more than anything their relationship had been, guilt more than the quality of the love itself, which had been brass at best and tarnished as well, and yet even knowing that he could not let go. For knowing that it was caused by guilt did not make the guilt go away.

Nothing had ever made the guilt go away.

He folded the shirt and put it back into the safe, then slammed the door shut.

He needed to start thinking about dinner.

3

It was a three-day drive, and less than ten minutes after merging onto I-40, beginning his long journey in earnest, he got a Violent Femmes tape stuck in his tape deck. By the time he pulled into a motel parking lot in downtown Louisville he must have listened to it forty times. Even after he killed the engine, silencing 'Kiss Off', he could hear the music bouncing around in his road-addled skull like a single coin in a Mason jar.

He sat, staring out his windshield at the sunset melting

across the jagged cityscape like an orange-flavored ice pop, and let himself come to terms with the silence. Eventually, the last echoes of the music faded away.

'Okay.'

He pushed open his door, stepped out into the evening, and almost fell to the asphalt. His right leg was cramping badly. You wouldn't think holding your foot down on a gas pedal would take much effort, and it didn't, but after three days his leg muscles were exhausted from being held in a single unnatural position. He rubbed at his thigh, cursing under his breath, and once he had massaged the cramp out of existence – though the pain did not fade completely – made his way toward the motel's front office.

He'd been wearing the same clothes since he left, eating nothing but shriveled gas-station hot dogs and barbecue-flavored corn chips, and sleeping in his car to save money despite the fact the backseat was cramped and near impossible to lie down in, even for a small man such as himself. Now that he was here he felt he needed a hot shower, a sit-down meal, and a night in an actual bed more than he'd ever needed any of those things before. They'd go a long way toward making him feel human again.

He pushed in through a glass door, a bell chiming as he did so, and a pretty black woman looked up from what she was doing – tapping away at the keyboard of an IBM computer – long enough to smile at him and say, 'Just a sec, hon.'

He nodded.

She finished what she was doing, removed a floppy disk from her machine, labeled it, put it away, and slid another floppy into place. Then she looked up at him and said, 'What can I do for you?'

'I just need a room for the night.'

'One bed?'

He nodded.

'Okay,' she said, glancing at a chart on the counter. 'Looks like room thirty-seven is available. It'll be forty-eight fifty.'

'You don't have anything cheaper?'

'I'm afraid not.'

'Is there any chance you can make it forty dollars even?'

'No, we can't do that, hon. We're busy in the summer.'

'But it's already evening and the room's empty.'

'I'm sorry.'

He sighed. 'All right. I'll take it.'

After he'd provided all the necessary information, she printed out an invoice on a dot-matrix printer, tore off the perforated edges, and handed it to him.

'Enjoy your stay. There's a free continental breakfast from seven to ten in the restaurant next door. Check-out time is eleven.'

Andrew stepped out of the shower feeling like himself for the first time in three days. While he got dressed he thought about driving by his father's house just to see if he could catch a glimpse of the man through a window, but he was too tired even to do that. The last thing in the world he wanted was to step into his car again.

Instead he walked to the hotel's restaurant/bar and took a seat at the counter. There were a few families sitting at tables, but he was the only person on a stool. The bartender, a hunch-backed fellow who looked like he might have lived through the Industrial Revolution, made eye contact and said: 'What can I do you for, young fellow?'

'Is it okay if I order food at the bar?'

The man nodded and handed him a menu. 'Take your time.'

He glanced down at the menu and said: 'I don't need to. I'll have a cheeseburger, a garden salad with ranch, and a Bud.'

'I need to see I.D.'

Andrew unpeeled the Velcro keeping his wallet secure and flipped his wallet open.

'Okay.' The bartender drew his beer, set it before him. 'I'll put your order in.'

Andrew nodded and took a sip of his beer.

What the hell was he doing here? He didn't know.

His father was a stranger – a stranger for whom he had nothing but hatred – and nothing good could come of this trip. Now that he was here, a mere ten miles from where his father lived and had lived for years, he realized that. Whatever he had hoped to get out of this journey when he began it he knew he would not. There was no peace here. There was no closure here. Closure comes from slamming a door shut, not from opening one. And what was he doing here but opening doors?

This trip was a mistake. He shouldn't be here. He couldn't stay.

Some doors are meant to remain closed. Some doors should be bricked over so they can never be opened again.

He would eat his dinner, get a good night's sleep, and start back home tomorrow morning. It was the only smart thing to do. He'd let his emotions control him to now, let some vague feeling in his gut bring him here, but the more he thought about what he was doing the more he realized it was a mistake. And not a small one. He needed to close the door on his past and simply live his life.

He needed to go home.

Next morning at half past eight he found himself sitting in his parked car in front of his father's bookshop, Dog-Eared Books. The place was closed and silent, the picture window reflecting the street back at him. Twin cars, powder-blue Pinto station wagons, rolled by, one of them on the street, the other reflected on the store's dark glass front.

He watched and waited. He didn't even know why he was here, didn't know what he was going to do. He'd made no plans. Was he even going to speak to the man?

He knew he shouldn't. He should start his car and get on the freeway.

He should start his car right now.

He steps from the car and walks across the street to the bookstore. He grabs the door handle and pulls. He steps into an air-conditioned room filled with shelves and piles of books. The stink of old books – cheap ink, glue – fills the air, reminding him of a youth spent in libraries. Hiding from bullies during summer vacation. Hiding from life in stories about crooked cops and unjust killings. He looks to his left and sees him standing behind the counter – his father. It's like looking into a cursed mirror. That is what he'll look like in another thirty-five years.

The man glances up at him. Says, can I help you, son? For a moment he panics. How does he know I'm his son? How the fuck does he know?

You look like him, that's how. Of course he'd recognize you.

But he doesn't. His face is blank-friendly, the face of a business owner who deals with customers daily. Probably he calls every young man who walks into the store the same thing.

He smiles at his father. Says, yeah, do you have any books on patricide?

The lights in the bookstore came on, allowing Andrew to see inside. Somehow he'd missed his father's arrival, but even now the man was shuffling about inside. He could see him in there – behind the glass, a mere ghost of a man, partially hidden by the reflected street, the two images overlaid – with his slumped shoulders and his gray hair, with his cardigan sweater and his khaki slacks.

For years he'd dreamed of this moment. His hands felt numb; his face tingled like a limb that had fallen asleep and felt hot with blood; his eyes stung. He had dreamed of this moment, but now it was here he didn't know what to do.

He did know what to do.

He pushes open his car door and steps out into the morning sunlight.

He sat in his car motionless.

He walks across the street and pushes into his father's bookstore.

He sat in his car motionless.

He looks at his father and his father looks back, making eye contact.

He sat in his car motionless.

His father pushed out of the store and stood a moment with his hands on his hips. He looked in Andrew's direction. Then he walked into the street, waited for traffic, and started toward him, moving at a brisk pace.

Andrew didn't know what to do. He looked at the keys hanging from the ignition, thought about starting his car and driving away, but the thought was a brief one. One thing he refused to do was run from this moment. Hadn't he driven three days to make this happen?

Yes, but you should turn around and go home.

Maybe, but I won't.

So it wasn't happening in any of the ways he'd imagined it might. That was life. It was happening still and he would not run from it.

He sat in his car and waited for his father to arrive.

He had no idea what might happen next, but that hardly seemed to matter. At least something was going to happen.

4

Harry was almost to his bookshop when he saw the kid sitting in the chrome-bumpered MGB GT. The car sat almost directly across the street from his bookshop and the kid was staring at said bookshop with a faraway look in his eyes. Harry brought his car to a stop in the street and watched the kid, glancing into his rearview mirror occasionally to make sure there was no one behind him. The kid didn't notice him. He just kept looking toward the bookshop, but not really. He was really looking into himself. That was obvious from his expression, the blank face of a person lost to the present world, traveling through the vast inner space of that mad pocket universe the mind.

Harry had a feeling the kid might have something to do with the private detective who'd shown up yesterday. He wasn't sure why he felt that. Perhaps it was only because the private detective was on his mind. But he didn't think so. He thought there was more to it.

Though that would have been enough, wouldn't it?

He pulled into the parking lot behind his shop and killed the engine. He stepped from his car and unlocked the back door. He propped open the door with a brick. He sat on his haunches and scratched Tom Selleck behind the ear, hearing his cat purr but paying the sound no mind. Really he was thinking about the kid parked across from his bookshop.

Why was he out there?

Why was he looking this way?

What was his mind doing behind those faraway eyes?

And who was he?

Harry got to his feet and walked to the counter. He looked through a box of books for no reason. He didn't know why he couldn't push himself forward, didn't know why his life was guided not by himself but by inertia. Even something as simple as inventorying and shelving books seemed daunting to him. It would require that he decide to do something and then actually do it – do it through force of will rather than as a simple twitch reaction.

Besides, he could think only of that kid parked out front. He knew there was no point in obsessing, but knowing that did not change the direction of his mind. It went where it wanted to go, thought of what it wanted to think of. What *he* wanted was irrelevant.

Probably the kid had nothing to do with anything. Probably he was thinking about the girlfriend he lost or something that happened at work the day before.

But that was bullshit, wasn't it? The car had California plates. He'd traveled a great distance to get to Louisville and he was looking at Harry's bookshop. Perhaps he was the person who'd hired that crooked private eye. But why? The only people he knew in California were his parents and his brother and his—

But it couldn't be.

The thought that his son might have tracked him down filled him both with joy and with dread. He had longed to be reunited with his son since the day he'd lost him, but there was so much between them that he'd always thought such a reunion impossible. Death and betrayal and abandonment: these were not things that people got over, nor were these things that people forgave. Harry hadn't even begun to forgive himself, so how could he expect his son to?

It probably wasn't even him. He'd seen California plates before and never thought such a thing, and there was no good reason for him to be thinking such a thing now. He was making connections where there were none. He was a tired old man letting his mind get away from him. That was all. The kid was just a kid, certainly not *his* kid. Probably he was out here for the summer visiting family after his first year at university on the west coast, or he'd moved here recently for work, or—

He was thinking about his own past because of the private detective's visit yesterday. His mind had been pushed in a certain direction and that was the direction it continued to travel. There couldn't possibly be anything more to it than that. Not after twenty-six years.

And yet—

He walked to the door and pulled it open.

He squinted at the little MGB across the street and the kid sitting behind the wheel. The kid looked back. They shared the same face. His was older, more worn out, but they shared the same face: the same eyes, the same mouth, the same chin, even the same hairline.

How could he have ever suspected that the boy was not his own?

What should he do? What *could* he do?

It didn't seem possible to turn around and head back into the store after he had seen what he had seen. It didn't make any sense to do such a thing. What if the kid started his engine and drove away? What if this was his only opportunity to make contact?

But what if his mind was playing tricks on him? He hadn't noticed the similarities earlier. He hadn't been looking for them earlier. What if he was seeing only what he wanted to see? That was a possibility. He'd spent years longing for a reunion he'd known impossible, so there was a very good chance that he was seeing similarities where there were none. He knew that after Helen's death he'd seen her everywhere – the back of a head that looked just like his wife's, a profile that could only be hers – yet every time he walked closer she disappeared and a new face emerged where hers should have been.

Because she was gone, as his son was gone.

It was true that the boy was not dead, but Harry

Combs was, had been for twenty-six years, and there could be no coming back from that.

Could there?

He waited for the street to clear and started across. He didn't know what he'd do or say, but he had to do or say something – unless, as he approached, the face became something different, something strange.

It almost had to, didn't it?

The features would morph as they came into focus, and the face would be nothing like his. Soon he'd be looking at a stranger. He was certain of it.

Almost certain.

He stopped only a few feet from the car and looked at the kid through the windshield. It almost *had* to be Andrew. Could anybody else have that face? He supposed it was possible, but there was no chance that that someone would be sitting outside his bookshop.

His son had tracked him down. His son had come to see him.

Harry raised a hand and held it there. Andrew did the same.

The driver side window was rolled down, so one of them could have spoken at any time, but for a long while neither of them did. Only silence filled the air between them.

Then Harry said: 'Why don't you come into the shop, have a cup of coffee?'

Andrew nodded and after an empty moment pushed open the door. He got to his feet.

Harry looked at him, his baby boy all grown up. The last time he'd seen him he was still in diapers. Now he was a young man. But this was really him, wasn't it? He still found it difficult to believe. And how could he have ever doubted Helen when she told him he was the father?

They walked toward the bookshop in silence.

When they arrived Harry opened the door and Andrew walked through it. Harry followed him in, letting the door swing shut behind him.

THEN:

Harry picks up the baby – his son – and looks toward the two corpses which lie on the burning carpet: his wife and the man who was once her lover. The flames lick at their flesh, and their flesh bubbles and turns black. The smell is strong and unpleasant and it fills his nostrils. He touches his bleeding head with his left hand. It throbs with pain. He finds it difficult to believe he's still alive, but doesn't know whether he's lucky or unlucky to have breath left in his lungs, thoughts in his head. Over the years he will have moments during which he believes both; it will depend on his mood; and each belief, though contradictory, will be accurate, life being what it is. He is both lucky and unlucky to be alive.

What the balance will be he'll know only upon his death.

Was it worth it?

He lifts the briefcase which lies at his feet and turns toward the door. He walks through the door, into the hallway, and tries to make his way to the front of the house. But he can no longer fight through the flames which are busy chewing up the curtains and the walls and the furniture and the floor. The heat is intense. He heads into the basement instead, his only option, trudging down the carpeted stairs, and can hear the crackling of wood above him and smell the scent of smoke pushing its way down between the floorboards. The smoke floats overhead, serpentine in its movements.

He walks through the damp-smelling basement toward the door, and as he does his eye catches a pile of laundry beside the washing machine, and atop that pile of laundry the shirt Helen wore on the evening they first met. The memory is so clear in his mind – her car rear-ending his; the way she stepped out indignantly saying you slammed on your brakes, you dumb motherfucker; the way he laughed at her anger; the way their eyes locked. It wasn't love at first sight – Harry doesn't believe in such a thing – but it sure was something. He picks up the shirt almost without thought, it's simply something he must keep, and walks to the exit, pushing open the door and making his way out into what was once his sunlit backyard, but which will now become just another place he left behind like so many others.

Out in front of the house, with his son in his arms, he scans the area. His Chevy Impala is parked across the street just a couple houses up. He walks to it and looks inside. The keys are still hanging from the ignition. He slides into the car and sets the baby in the passenger seat. He sets the briefcase on the floor and Helen's blue shirt on top of it.

He starts the engine.

*

He holes up in a motel just outside Houston for three days, not knowing what to do, not knowing what his next move should be. He thinks of Helen and cries. He takes care of his son as well as he can, though sometimes the baby's wailing gets to be too much and he sits in the bathtub staring at the faucet while in the other room the noise continues unabated. Sometimes he manages to take in a meal, though almost as often he vomits. He isn't sure if it's from his head injury or what he experienced in the house. If he could he'd see a doctor. He knows he should. His head aches constantly, throbs constantly, and the wound is still seeping blood. He's been having dreams of men hitting him with hammers, of boulders crushing his skull, of vises closing down on him.

He considers going back to Dallas and taking care of everyone who got him into this mess. He could send his son to California, grandma and grandpa would take care of him, and head back to Dallas to wipe every one of those motherfucking smudges out of existence. Just thumb them all out. Lord knows they have it coming.

Except he doesn't think he could do it.

He doesn't think he has that in him anymore. He feels broken. He feels soft and weak and lost and entirely without direction, and in order to do what he'd have to do in Dallas he'd need direction. He'd need direction and he'd need drive.

What he really wants to do is fold up into himself like a camping chair and sleep for six months, perhaps a year. He wants to wake up and have all of this behind him – far behind him.

He can't go back to Dallas. They'd kill him before he got close. Not if he was his old self, but being who he is now, soft and weak, they'd kill him.

He has a quarter-million dollars in a briefcase. He can simply disappear. He can get away. He can change his name and become a new person. He needs to become a new person. Maybe he can even have a life with his son, watch him grow up, see the resemblance between him and Helen and take some small comfort in the fact that at least a part of her lives on in her beautiful son, in their beautiful son, in his eyes and his—

But of course the boy cannot come with him. Harry's wanted dead. It doesn't matter where he goes. They'll look for him. Eventually they might catch up with him. Maybe the chances aren't great, but they're more than negligible. And if they do catch up with him, and if his son is there, he will be as responsible for the boy's death as he is for Helen's.

He needs to send the boy to California.

And then, like a magician, he needs to disappear: poof. Goodbye, everyone. That's his only option. It will mean losing everything, it will mean losing even his son, but that's the price he must pay to keep the boy safe. That's all there is to it. He must keep his son safe.

His losses are irrelevant. What it means to him is irrelevant.

He calls a friend in Dallas, a woman he had a brief affair with before he met Helen – he comforted her after her husband, an associate of his, took two to the back of the head in a dark alley – and asks her to drive out to Houston and meet him at a diner on Westheimer Road. He knows it's a risk calling anyone from his old life, but he doesn't see that he has a choice.

She pauses for a long time after he makes his request. The silence stretches out between them, and he knows if it goes on much longer, if he allows it to go on much longer, the next word spoken will be no, and once she says it her mind will be made up.

He can't allow that to happen.

It's very important, Barbara, he says. You know I wouldn't be calling if it wasn't.

She asks him what's going on, is it true about Helen, is it true what the police are saying you did to Helen.

It isn't true, not all of it is, but I can't discuss that right now. I need you to tell me you'll come out here and meet with me – please.

Eventually she says she'll do it. He hangs up the phone and puts his forehead against the wall and stands there for some time with his eyes closed. He tries to think of nothing. He fails, of course, but he tries.

After a few minutes he walks to the bed and gets on his hands and knees. He reaches into the darkness and retrieves a black briefcase. He sets it on the bed, unlatches it, opens it, and within finds stack after stack of hundred-dollar bills. He removes a ten-thousand-dollar bundle and tosses it onto the mattress, then closes the briefcase once more, drops it to the floor, kicks it under the bed.

He's got a little over five hours to wait before Barbara arrives.

He sits nervously in a booth at the diner sipping coffee and feeling like he might vomit. His son sits in a wooden high chair sipping apple juice from a glass bottle. He looks out the window watching cars pass by and thinking of his life going down the drain of the world. He thinks of trying to start a new life and wonders if that will be possible. He doesn't see how. Everything he ever loved has been or is being taken from him. Where do you go when you have nothing left, when you have nothing more to care about?

He doesn't know.

He doesn't know how he's going to force himself forward when he has only himself to care about – because he doesn't care about himself at all. He hates himself. He hates both what he is and what he was. He wouldn't care if the ground opened up and swallowed him whole. He's hurt or killed everyone he ever loved, everyone who ever loved him.

A rush of pain flows through his head. He closes his eyes and pinches the bridge of his nose and hopes it subsides. He knows it won't go away completely – it's been constant since his last day in Dallas – but it's making his eyes water, making it hard to think, so he hopes it fades once more to the background.

Or that the wound finally kills him.

That would be okay too. It might even be for the best.

The diner's front door swings open.

He looks up.

Barbara walks into the place, thin and beautiful as always, wearing a narrow blue dress that somehow makes her look even thinner than she is. She scans the room, looking for him.

He holds up a hand and tries to smile through the pain.

After a moment she spots him and walks over but does not return the smile. She slides onto the bench seat across from him and immediately lights a cigarette, her lipstick staining the white filtered tip. She exhales smoke in a thin stream and looks at him.

'It's good to see you, Barb,' he says.

'I wish I could say the same.'

He nods.

'What is it you want?'

He motions toward his son.

'What about him?'

'I want you to take him to his grandparents in California.'

'What?'

'He isn't safe with me.'

Before the sentence is even out of his mouth she's shaking her head.

'I can pay you, Barb.'

'It isn't about money, Harry. I don't want to get involved.'

'You don't have *to get involved. Just take him to his grandparents.'*

'I'm sorry.'

'I can pay you ten thousand dollars. I know you could use

it. Dylan didn't leave you with much, and Rathbone is not a generous man to the families of those whose lives he's used up. Take the money and do this for me. I know you need it, and I need you.'

Harry stands in the parking lot and watches Barbara drive away with his son, and when they're out of view he knows he now truly does have nothing. Everyone he's ever loved is gone.

Hell, he'll never even be able to see Barbara again. She's been nothing more than someone he 'used to know' for a long time – though he's often thought of her quirks: of how she once ate nothing but rotisserie chicken for six months straight, until when her appendix burst doctors found chicken in it; of how she seemed to collect wooden spoons for no good reason, filling drawers and jars in her kitchen; of her strange fits of madness – but now even the slight chance that he will see her again is gone. She was not important to him – or rather, she was important to him only for a brief time years ago – but the fact that he can't see even her again makes it all feel very real.

He can see no one from his old life ever again, not even the incidental people.

It feels terrible and empty – there is nothing in him now but a great sucking hollow; his heart is a mud pit – but, oddly, there's something liberating about it too. If you have nothing you are *nothing, and if you are nothing you have the potential to be anything, for there are no distinguishing characteristics which limit the possibilities. He no longer has to be Harry*

Combs. He no longer has to be this man he has grown to hate. He can become something different. He can become something good.

For a long moment he thinks about that, and he wonders if it's true – if he really can become something good after all the harm he's done – and then, when he's done thinking about it, at least for the moment, he walks to his car.

NOW:

1

Andrew sat across from his father and stared at him. They both sat in silence for a very long time, sizing up one another. They sat with the same slouched posture, one hand on the arm of a chair, the other holding a paper cup of coffee. They wore the same expressionless faces. Andrew knew it without having to see himself – he'd seen his own reflection enough – and he hated it, hated it because it reminded him once more that he was merely a younger version of this man he despised, this man who had cold-bloodedly murdered his mother twenty-six years before and left him an orphan.

And yet looking at his father he also felt something like sympathy. There was a sad desperation in his rheumy red eyes, a pathetic need for acceptance that floated right on the surface like so much flotsam, a need for love, and that look in his eyes contradicted Andrew's perception of the man. How could someone capable of shooting his own wife in the head – shooting and killing both her and her lover – how could such a man have that look in his eyes? And even if that was a crime of passion, something done in the moment, he was also a man who had cold-bloodedly murdered strangers with forethought and without apparent remorse – for he'd done it more than once. It didn't make any sense, then, that he should have such a look in his eyes. He should be emotionless, as cold as his actions, as cold as a winter stone.

But then people were contradictory. Everyone had at least two different personalities within them, sometimes more, and each of those personalities was further complicated by mood and circumstance. A woman could drown her children in the bathtub and cry at the accidental loss of a pet. A man could beat his wife and be a sweet father, or beat his children and be a loving husband. There was no telling with people. You just never knew what contradictory things might be contained within the skin of a single human.

Killers might need love as much as anybody.

Finally, his father spoke: 'You look well.'

'Thank you.'

It seemed odd that with so much between them those two sentences should be the beginning of their conversation. But he supposed it also made sense. Where else do you start? Where else *can* you start? You must work your way to the heart by first picking at the surface. You never start in deep, no matter what has happened; you must dig your way in.

'I've dreamed of this,' his father said. 'I've dreamed of getting to see you again. I never thought it would happen, but I hoped.'

'I've thought about it a lot, too.'

He looks to his right and sees a letter opener on the counter beside a stack of mail. He stands up and grabs it. The metal handle is cool in his sweaty palm and he can feel the design etched into it rough against his skin. He grips it tight and turns toward his father. He stands still a moment, then lunges at the man, sinking the letter opener into his neck while thinking, you motherfucker. You killed my mother. You killed my mother and then you vanished. He lets go the handle and takes a step back. His father looks at him with acceptance in his eyes, acceptance and complete understanding. The letter opener juts from his neck – inexplicably making Andrew think of a coat hook – and blood bubbles out around the blade thick and somehow frothy.

He glanced right and saw a letter opener on the counter beside a stack of mail, but he did not move. He remained in his chair, his body tense.

The light leaves his father's eyes and his head drops down. Blood soaks into his sweater and the shirt beneath it. Andrew feels a strange sense of relief. He is free. He is free of the burden he has been living with his entire life. With one swing of the arm, with one quick incision, he has managed to shed his father's skin. The man is dead, yet he is not. The man is dead

73

while he still breathes – he can feel air entering his lungs even now – so they were different people after all. And now he can finally become himself.

He turned away from the letter opener and back toward his father.

And now he can finally become himself.

'Have you?'

'I have,' Andrew said, 'for years.'

Tears streamed down his father's cheeks and he put his right hand to his face, rubbing at his eyes with index finger and thumb. His entire body shook with emotion.

'I'm so sorry,' he said. 'I'm so sorry, son.'

Andrew looks to his right and sees a letter opener on the counter beside a stack of mail.

2

'Then why did you do it?'

Harry looked up, wiping the tears away from his eyes. He blinked at the window for a moment, trying to collect himself, watching the cars on Bardstown Road roll by, watching pedestrians stroll along the sidewalks. Such a difficult question Andrew had asked him – a fair question, of course, but the answer was not a simple one.

He looked at his son and his son looked back, giving him nothing. His expression was cold, unfeeling. He'd turned himself off. Harry knew it just by looking at him.

There'd been a time in his life when he was capable of doing that too. It was a necessary part of his job. Like flipping a switch you turn yourself off, kiss emotion goodbye – see you on the other side, buddy – and you cease to feel anything. Then all you're left with is your brain, and an intelligent person can rationalize anything, even murder. You analyze a situation like a scientist, like a mathematician.

You don't let heart get in the way.

You lie in the prone position on a rooftop and watch through your scope as a man walks out of a bank. His pig-tailed six-year-old is with him and they're holding hands, but you don't let that get to you. You don't let anything get to you. This isn't about that man, nor is it about his daughter. It's about nothing but the algebra of blood, and the math says this man will die today. That's all. You don't ask why. There is no why. There is what and there is how and there is who, and you're about to make the what happen, and this is how you do it, and this is who you do it to. You wait for your moment. The man pauses at a crosswalk. You squeeze the trigger and before the man even has a chance to hear the report he's down, leaving a red mist in the air where his head once was. His daughter stands there a moment confused, her face and dress covered in blood and little shards of bone and small gelatinous bits of brain. Then she starts to scream. But it's nothing to you. It isn't as if you haven't heard the sound of screaming before; it isn't as if you won't hear it again.

'It's not as simple as that,' he said.

'It is.'

Harry shook his head.

'It didn't happen how you think it happened.'

'I don't believe you.'

'I know what people think. I'm sure you think the same thing. There's no reason you wouldn't. Maybe you've even read newspaper articles about it. The police had it solved within twenty-four hours. But it didn't happen like that.'

His son repeated himself: 'I don't believe you.'

Harry nodded, resigned.

Why would the boy believe him?

The world knew the truth of what he was. Who was he to argue?

It almost felt pointless to discuss what had happened. His son wasn't asking what happened; he was asking why it happened. He didn't know yet that there was no why. He didn't know yet that there never *is* a why – not one that matters, anyway, not one that brings sense to everything. You cannot pull back from reality and see the big picture as astronauts see the earth from space.

All you get are small moments.

Little details.

And sometimes things just happen. You want there to be a reason. You want to know your son came home from a foreign land in a body bag because he was fighting for freedom. You want him to be a hero. You want your mother's cancer to be part of God's plan. You want her to be in a better place. But that isn't the way it is.

What happened was that they died, and that's all that happened.

Maybe a child with an IED walked up to his platoon. Maybe the cancer metastasized to her bones and her liver.

But there's no why.

The why of a story is always mere fairy tale.

He could still, however, give his son the how and the what and the who, despite the fact that he seemed not to want to hear it. He could tell his son those details, and maybe that would be enough. He didn't think it would be – he didn't even think his son would believe him – but he could try. What did he have to lose by trying?

Yet as he opened his mouth and began speaking he found himself telling less than the complete truth. He found himself unable to say everything.

There were things he'd done he knew his son would hate him for, and now that his son was here sitting across from him he couldn't bear the thought of being hated by him. So he left things out; he bent the truth. He didn't quite bend the truth to its breaking point – he told himself he didn't, anyway – but he came very close.

His son sat in silence and listened to his story.

3

Andrew listened to his father lie. Listened to him tell an elaborate story about being part of a four-man crew involved in a political assassination in November 1963. Listened to him talk about how the men involved were then getting picked off one by one the following spring. Listened to him say he never knew exactly why Rathbone went after them but assumed it was his way of tying up loose ends. The man behind the curtain could not be revealed, and if any of the crew were to be caught that could lead right back to him, which was apparently a risk he was unwilling to take. Or perhaps it was a risk the even more powerful men who hired him to get the job done were unwilling to take. Either way, after the first two men were killed, his father knew he was looking at a clean-up job rather than an isolated event, and knowing this knew he had to get out of town – had to get hundreds or thousands of miles from town – or die.

And death was not an option. It was always a possibility, of course, but he would not choose it. He would not stand still while it walked toward him scythe in hand. He needed to disappear, but in order to disappear – in order to disappear effectively – he had to get his hands on some money. He and his family would need new identities, which were not cheap, and they'd need road money, and funds to set up a new life once they felt safe enough to settle down somewhere. If they lit out for the territories taking with them only what they had they were much more likely to be caught. If you hope to survive you need resources, and money is the ultimate resource in an urban world: it will provide all the others.

Though he'd never held up a bank, that was his first thought. It wasn't ideal, of course. In fact, it was far from ideal. He'd have to put together a crew and split funds he desperately needed. But it was a quick way to get his hands on cash, if he was lucky, and he didn't have time for anything more elaborate or subtle.

The problem – the big problem – was that it was very likely to put the police onto him, which would make disappearing all the more difficult. He'd had enough troubles with the law over the years and didn't want any now.

Then he heard that the fourth man on the crew, a man he disliked for reasons he'd rather not go into, had pulled a job of his own. He hadn't held up a bank. Instead he'd decided to steal from the man who wanted him dead. Broke into the building, blew the safe, and walked away with a briefcase full of cash. And why not? He couldn't be killed twice.

Andrew interrupted him here with: 'This was Paul Watkins.'

His father shook his head and said: 'No. Paul Watkins came later.'

'Mom had an affair with him.'

After a long pause his father nodded. 'But that was

more than two years before his involvement in what happened in Dallas – and unrelated.'

'That's why you killed them.'

'No.'

'You killed them for that and the money.'

'That isn't how it happened.'

Andrew didn't know if his father's story about being involved in a political assassination was true, but he doubted it. Such an assassination in Dallas at that time could mean only one thing, and he found it almost impossible to believe his father had been on the grassy knoll. It made his chest feel tight. The absolute *wrongness* of the thought made him want to reject it without consideration. And if his father was not involved in said assassination it was also unlikely that someone was trying to kill him. The first thing led to the second and if the first hadn't happened – well, then, that was that.

The only fact he knew for certain was that Paul Watkins, his mother's lover, stole at least a quarter-million dollars from an organized crime operation in Dallas and was going to take that money and his mother away from there. He was going to take her, the money, and her eighteen-month-old son. They'd get away from Harry Combs and all that he represented. They'd get away from the violence and the danger and set up a peaceful life far away from there.

They could have lived as a happy family in a pastel-painted beach house in Florida, taking the boat out on weekends or grilling steaks in the backyard. Or perhaps they could have lived in a farmhouse in some rural backwoods in Idaho, raising pigs for slaughter and eating big meals at the tableclothed oak dining table.

Had either of those things happened Andrew would be a different person. But they didn't happen. His father stopped all possibilities with the pull of a trigger, stopped them with a bullet. But one wasn't enough for him, so he pulled the trigger twice.

His father looked down at his lap and ran a finger along the crease ironed into his pants. He picked at a loose piece of thread, balled it between index finger and thumb, flicked it to the carpeted floor.

He looked up and made eye contact. 'Maybe we shouldn't discuss this.'

'I want to.'

'You already think you know what happened.'

'I *do* know what happened.'

'You don't,' his father said, 'and you won't believe what I tell you.'

'Then don't lie. Do you really believe I could hate you more than I already do?'

4

Harry did not believe what he next said – he knew all the way down to his bones that what he said was a lie – but he wanted his son to be his son again, and he didn't know how else to make it happen. He didn't even know if what he was about to say would make it happen, he doubted it, but it was better than the truth. He could not admit that he was the only one responsible for his wife's death. He could not admit that if he had been a different person, a better person, she would now be alive. He could not admit these things *aloud*, despite the fact he had admitted them to himself long ago. So he told his son something he did not believe. He told him that George Rathbone was responsible for Helen's death.

Rathbone was the man behind the curtain. Everybody knew it but no one could prove it.

Or rather: no one *wanted* to prove it; no one in the state of Texas, anyway.

Many people, important people, could have made any number of serious claims, and many of them could have provided evidence to back up their claims, but none of them would. He was an important man, a man willing to grease the Texas political machine with green, and therefore he was protected. He was untouchable.

If a senator was elected in Texas it was because Rathbone wanted him elected, and if a businessman in serious debt was killed outside a bank in front of his six-year-old daughter, well, that was because Rathbone wanted him dead.

And now Rathbone wanted Harry dead.

Even protected men knew their first line of defense was protecting themselves.

That was why he had to go on the run.

He needed to pack up and leave before Rathbone caught up with him and put him in a shallow grave somewhere – he needed to protect his family – and the first step in doing this was to get the money the fourth man in their crew had stolen from Rathbone. At the time he was hearing rumors that it was anywhere from a hundred grand to a million dollars, but even the smaller sum would be more than enough for his purposes. He almost *hoped* it was the smaller sum; that would give Rathbone less incentive to hunt him down.

But first, of course, he had to get his hands on it.

THEN:

Harry tracks Cecil Leroy down to a seedy motel on West North-
west Highway, the kind of place that, in the evening, had
prostitutes hanging out in front of it under unlighted street
lamps and a parking lot with at least a couple tractor trailers
clogging its spaces. He parks and walks around the building,
looking for Cecil's most likely escape route. He's going to be
nervous, twitchy, being wanted dead by Rathbone, which
means that if there's a knock at the door he's unlikely to
answer. His answering would, in fact, be a fucking miracle.

Probably he'll go straight for his window.

He finds Cecil's car – a banged-up Buick – parked behind
the building and removes an ivory-handled fold-out knife from
his pocket. He thumbs it open and walks to the vehicle. He sits
on his haunches and sticks the knife into rubber, twisting it as
best he can against the thick material's resistance. The tire
hisses as air escapes.

He does this three more times to three more tires before

walking back around to the front of the building. He pauses before Cecil's door. He looks through the peephole and sees movement on the other side, a dark shadow. He raises his fist. He bangs hard on the door and without waiting for an answer he thinks unlikely to come runs again toward the back of the building.

As he turns the corner he sees Cecil Leroy, shirtless, pants unbuttoned, climbing through his window frantically. The man's bare feet hit the ground. He stumbles forward, falls, dropping a black briefcase, picks himself back up. He reaches down and grabs the briefcase. A breeze catches his blond hair which waves like grass.

Harry runs after him.

Cecil hears the footsteps coming up behind him and looks over his shoulder. Then he's darting toward his car.

He must be in such a panic that he doesn't notice the flat tires, because he runs around the back of it, pulls the door open, falls into the vehicle. He starts the engine.

But by now Harry is upon him.

He thrusts the blade through the open window and into Cecil's sternum. There's a strange popping noise as the blade punctures bone, then it slides in easily.

Cecil's foot leaves the brake pedal and the car of its own volition rolls backward, the tires making a strange flopping sound. It turns slightly as it rolls, then thuds into a cinderblock wall and ceases to move, though the engine rumbles on.

Harry stabs Cecil seven more times before removing the blade and wiping it off on the man's Levi's. He pockets it. Then he walks to the passenger side and pulls open the door. He picks up the briefcase and walks once more toward the front of the building. But he does not run. The best way to walk away from a crime scene is calmly. You didn't do a thing – hell, you didn't even see a thing.

He slides into his car, tossing the briefcase onto his own passenger seat, and sticks his key into the ignition. He turns the key and pumps the gas pedal. After a stressful ten seconds – his carburetor needs work – the engine roars to life. He backs out of the parking spot and heads toward the street.

As he's leaving the driveway, he sees Paul Watkins pulling in.

Paul turns his head and looks at him.

For a moment they simply sit in their cars making eye contact.

Of all the shit-luck timing.

Harry jams his foot down on the gas pedal and swerves into traffic.

As he screeches left around the next corner, he glances into his sideview mirror and sees Paul Watkins's car roaring down the street after him. He's got to think of a way to get rid of this guy. He's got to end him.

That's his only option.

The man is a machine and won't stop until he's dead – which suits Harry fine. The man tried to steal his wife away from him, almost succeeded in stealing his wife away from him

– and possibly fathered the child Harry is raising as his own, though his doubts sometimes put a knot in his stomach and make his chest feel tight – and the fact that it's been just over two years – two years and three months – since it happened has not made Harry's anger fade.

If Harry weren't afraid of Rathbone's reaction, he'd have killed Paul Watkins years ago. He'd have killed him when he found out about the affair. The man had stained Harry's relationship with Helen, stole away the trust he had for her – the only woman he'd ever trusted – and in doing so had stolen from him what he'd once thought was the most important relationship in his life. If a man didn't deserve to die for that he didn't deserve to die for anything. You do not fuck with what another man holds sacred, and while Harry does not believe in an afterlife or God, he does believe in love.

It's the only *thing he believes in, despite Helen's betrayal.*

He turns right, screeching around another corner, white smoke rising hot from the asphalt before the wind breaks the clouds apart and carries them away.

He looks in his rearview mirror.

The car giving chase hooks around the corner fishtailing wildly, straightens out, and continues on.

This has to end. It has to end now.

Harry slams on his brakes and turns down an alley. He drives to a chain-link fence and yanks up on the parking brake. He jumps the fence and runs around a red brick building, huffing for air, a sharp pain stabbing at his left side.

When he reaches the alley once more from the front, Paul

Watkins's car is parked there behind his own, blocking it in, and Watkins is looking at it. A revolver hangs from his large pale hand. He steps around his own car door and toward Harry's vehicle, then he takes another step, and another. He reaches the open door and leans in to grab the black briefcase.

Harry thumbs open his fold-out knife. He wishes like hell he'd brought his automatic pistol. He wishes like hell he'd thought ahead and prepared. But he hadn't expected to have to deal with Watkins. He'd planned only on handling Cecil Leroy, a punk, and anyway one didn't want to fire a pistol in the vicinity of an occupied motel, even one as seedy as the place Leroy was staying: too many people around to hear the shots.

Well, fuck it. He's done what he's done and must live with it – unless he's to die with it.

He walks up behind Paul Watkins, stepping as softly as possible, and is almost upon the man when his right foot grinds against a shard of broken glass from a shattered beer bottle.

Paul Watkins spins around, raising his revolver.

Harry grabs the man's wrist and thrusts it away just as the gun goes off. The bullet hits brick and red flakes of baked clay fly off the building.

Harry swings his knife-hand toward Watkins's ribcage, hoping like hell it strikes home, hoping like hell it slips its way between the bones and into an organ, any fucking organ at all, but instead Paul drops the briefcase and blocks it, wrenches his gun-hand free, and brings the thing down against the side of Harry's head.

He stumbles backward, but manages to keep from falling.

When he once more looks at Paul Watkins the man's gun is aimed at his face.

So this is it, then: he's done what he's done and he's to die with it.

NOW:

1

After his father finished speaking the room went silent. Andrew sipped his coffee, not because he was thirsty but because it gave him time to think, and he needed time to think. He needed time to figure out just how much of his father's story he believed: something close to half – perhaps a bit less.

Though even the things he didn't fully believe bothered him. What if they were true? What if his father was involved in a political assassination? What if George Rathbone really had sent Paul Watkins to kill the people involved in said assassination?

What if – what if he was the son, not of Harry Combs, but of Paul Watkins? Would that mean he'd spent his entire life filled with pointless hatred? Would that mean his spleen was misdirected even now? But those were worthless questions. Harry Combs had still murdered his mother. Harry Combs had still made him an orphan – in one way or another.

When Andrew looked in the mirror he saw the resemblance. He was his father's son and his father was Harry Combs.

Looking at the man he knew this to be true.

And he understood the lies, understood the desperation behind them, but that understanding did not create within him any sympathy for the man. He had gained some understanding, yes, but he hated his father nonetheless. In a strange way his understanding had worked to increase his hatred. He could empathize with his father after all because he was like him – because he *was* his father's son – because he would have told the same lies had he been in this situation, and because this made him hate himself it made him hate his father all the more.

It made him want to shed this skin so badly.

In his heart – where he still knew what his mind might doubt – he wanted to be free.

But when he finally spoke he spoke but one word: 'Okay.'

His father looked at him in confusion. 'I don't understand.'

'I believe you.'

With those words his father's face changed. His eyes did not become brighter. His mouth did not shift. His crow's feet did not crinkle with some faint smile. There would be no way to describe what happened in detail, for there were no details to describe; it was simply as if the shadow of a cloud which had lain upon him finally passed, allowing the sunlight to hit his skin once more.

It was almost beautiful to watch, but even that made Andrew hate his father. The man did not deserve beauty, neither to possess it nor to view it.

He deserved nothing but pain.

2

Harry looked at his son in both relief and disbelief. Andrew had hated him at the beginning of this conversation, and rightly so – how could he not hate him, believing what he believed? – but somehow his words had worked. Somehow, without asking for it, he'd been forgiven. He hoped that was the case, anyway; he wanted it to be true more than he'd wanted anything in a very long time, and that was the implication of his son's words. Without saying it he was saying it: I forgive you.

'How long will you be in town?'

Andrew shrugged. 'I don't know. I hadn't thought about it. Just knew I had to see you.'

'You should stay a couple weeks if you can. We've lost so much time.'

A strange look passed over his son's face with those words. It was there only briefly, too briefly to read fully, and then it was gone, and though Harry didn't know exactly what it meant it had not been the look of someone who'd forgiven him. It had not even been the look of someone who'd *believed* him. There was anger there. There was utter *rage*.

He told himself to stop. He told himself to take his son at his word. If his son could listen to what he'd told him and accept it he could at the very least believe that his son *did* in fact accept it. It was the only way for them to move forward from here. He could not second-guess everything and hope for a positive outcome too.

Finally his son spoke: 'I think that's a good idea.'

'I'm so glad to hear it. Can I – can I hug you?'

His son stiffened and inhaled through his nose.

After some time he said: 'I think we'll have to wait on that.'

Harry nodded. 'That's fine,' he said. 'I understand.'

Which was true: it hurt some but he understood. Probably he shouldn't have asked. It was too much too soon. They'd have to take things one step at a time, and today, this morning, they'd already taken a very large step indeed. They'd taken the biggest, most important step. They'd spoken for the first time. When last he saw his boy the child was capable of only a few simple words, and even those he barely managed.

Now he was a man.

Harry thought about what that meant. He thought

about time. He thought about how it moves forward whether or not you move forward with it.

Maybe he should step back into the flow of things.

3

His father invited him to sleep in the guest bedroom and he accepted the invitation, not because he wanted to but because he didn't have money to spend on a motel, and also because he thought it would get him closer to his ends, it would help him to accomplish what he needed to accomplish before heading home, and the sooner that happened, the better.

Unfortunately, he still didn't know what it was he hoped to accomplish. All he knew was that something more needed to happen. He felt it in the pit of his stomach. This wasn't over; it was barely begun.

He slid behind the wheel of his MGB and started the engine, pumping the gas pedal to keep it running until it smoothed out, and when his father pulled out of the store's driveway and made a left onto Bardstown Road he stabbed the thing into first and pulled back on the clutch, darting into the street behind him.

He followed the man down Bardstown until the next light, where they made a left. Then another left onto Norris, after which he lost his sense of place and simply followed the car in front of him along a series of twisting side streets.

They pulled to a stop in front of a two-storey brick Cape Cod. Paint was peeling from the concrete porch. A dilapidated swing creaked in the hot summer breeze. Flowers poked dead from window boxes.

He stepped out of the MGB as his father stepped out of his car and they met at the concrete steps which led up the steep ivy-covered front yard to the green-painted front door.

'I apologize for Teresa in advance.'

'Your wife?'

'She has a bit of a drinking problem.'

Then his father keyed open the door and they went inside.

His father's wife was asleep when they went into the kitchen. She was sitting in a wooden chair, her head resting upon the dining-room table. An empty vodka bottle sat beside her head. A broken glass lay shattered on the floor.

His father picked up a broom which leaned against the wall beside the trash can and went about sweeping up the broken glass. Once a neat pile was formed he scooped the glass into a dust pan and dumped it into the trash bin, and when that was done he walked to his wife and touched her shoulder gently.

'Teresa,' he said.

She shifted in her sleep but did not awaken.

He shook her again.

Her eyes fluttered, then opened red and glossy. She sat up, a mark on her cheek from where it had rested on the table. She blinked several times.

'Harry.' She smiled.

'Let's get you into bed.'

'That's a – that's a good idea.'

She tried to push herself off the table and to her feet but was only about halfway up when her hand slipped out from under her. It swung against the vodka bottle and knocked it over. She dropped back into the chair and a grunt escaped her. The bottle rolled off the edge of the table, but his father managed to grab it mid-fall, gotcha, and set it down upright.

'Should we try again?'

His wife nodded.

'Okay,' he said, 'let me help.'

He leaned forward and scooped his arms under her armpits. He lifted her to her feet. She swayed a moment, threatened to go down, then regained her balance. A smile touched her lips and she kissed him and said I love you very much, Harry White. He flinched away from the stink of her breath – at least that's how Andrew perceived it – but said I love you too, honey. Then he guided her down a hallway, being very gentle, very loving. She swayed as she walked, but his support did not waver.

Watching this Andrew felt once more confusion in reaction to the contradiction between his preconceived notions about his father and the man as he lived and breathed. This was the person he'd spent his life despising? This sad and gentle man with his sad and simple life?

But it was, and seeing the man as he lived and breathed did not make Andrew hate him any less, for he knew what he contained within him despite his outward appearance. He knew what the man was capable of. People did not change. They were who they were; they were *what* they were. Sometimes, maybe always, they contained contradictions. Evil people could have moments of kindness, moments of vulnerability, but that did not make them any less evil.

The man had murdered his wife and abandoned his son. That he was capable of being gentle and kind did not change that. It only put into relief the way he had treated Andrew's mother and Andrew himself. Was his mother not worthy of forgiveness? Was he not worthy of kindness? Were neither of them worthy of the love of which this man was clearly capable?

They were.

If his father believed they weren't he was wrong.

Why wouldn't they be worthy of that? Why the fuck *wouldn't* they?

His father returned to the kitchen looking rather embarrassed.

'Sorry about that,' he said.

'It's fine.'

'It's not.'

'It isn't so bad.'

'It is,' his father said. 'It is – but I love her.'

Andrew did not respond.

4

Harry dug through the fridge trying to find something to cook for dinner. He wished he'd stopped at Kroger on the way home, or made a trip out to Kingsley Meat and Seafood. He wanted to make steak or lobster. He wanted to make something that reflected how he felt about this evening. He was about to eat a meal with his son for the first time in twenty-six years.

Unfortunately he had only a few catfish filets. He breaded them with crushed cornflakes, salt and pepper, and fried them up while cooking peas in butter and baking frozen french fries. His son sat and watched him in silence.

When the meal was done he prepared three plates and walked back to the bedroom to awaken Teresa. She'd been asleep in bed for over an hour now, but would still be drunk. He hoped, however, that she would not be too embarrassing.

He wanted the evening to go well.

5

Andrew sat at the dinner table with a plate of hot food in front of him. He looked to his left. Teresa sat drunkenly before her own plate. She'd been staring down at her lap, but when Andrew looked toward her she lifted her head and smiled at him. He smiled back, but doubted very much that his smile appeared genuine. His eyes felt dead in their sockets, lifeless as belly-up fishes. He looked to his right. His father was looking back, expressionless, simply watching the wordless interaction between his son and his wife. His father said nothing either, only watched. Then dropped his head, cut a piece of fish with his fork, took a bite. Andrew wondered briefly what was going through his father's head, then decided he didn't care.

He picks up his own fork and examines it – the shining metal, the sharp prongs, the hard-water spots on the handle. He feels its weight in his hand. It's certainly heavy enough to be used as a weapon. He grips it tight and looks toward his father once more. Then, and without warning, he thrusts the fork toward his father's face. He plunges it into his father's head and the man jerks back. His chair tilts, threatens to fall, then does fall, and his father falls with it. He lands on his back and rolls onto his side, grabbing at the fork in his eye. He screams as he pulls it out and drops it to the floor. Bits of eye cling to it, stringy and moist, like steamed-off tomato skin. Blood pours down his face from his empty eye socket and puddles on the linoleum floor beneath his head.

Andrew set his fork down, picked up a couple french fries. He dipped them into tartar sauce and shoved them into his mouth. He chewed them without tasting them. They had the texture of wet cardboard.

'The tartar sauce is very good,' he said.

His father smiled at him.

6

Harry lay awake in bed staring at the cracked ceiling. He thought about his son and wondered what his son was thinking as he lay fifteen feet away in the guest bedroom. He wondered if he was thinking anything at all. Maybe he wasn't. Maybe he was asleep and dreaming – but dreaming of what? What kind of scenes might be playing themselves out on the inside of his eyelids? Perhaps he was dreaming of a boy without a father, or of a woman dead in a burning house, her brains ejected from a conical hole in the back of her head, her skin bubbling and cracking as the boiling fluids leaked out from within her.

He reached out and grabbed Teresa's hand in his own and squeezed it.

He thought about the private detective he was to give ten thousand dollars to tomorrow. He was certain his son was responsible for this man's presence in his life – it was the only thing that made sense – but he didn't care. Or rather, he didn't blame the boy. He'd view the blackmail as payment for getting his son back. He'd happily pay double that amount and more. What did bother him was that the man knew his secret, that the man knew his other name and everything that clung to it heavy as lead. His mind kept turning to that fact. Again and again he'd think about it. It bothered him that there was someone out there who could destroy his life at any time. He'd worked so hard to become Harry White and yet twenty-six years later Harry Combs was still there, still haunting him, the ghost of the man he once was.

He was irrevocably chained to him whether he wanted to be or not.

He thought about killing the private detective, thought about it seriously, thought about it beyond mere ideation. It would break at least one of the chains that connected him to his former self. He thought about how he would do it. He thought about whether he'd do it quietly and simply dispose of the body or do it from a distance and vanish from the scene. He was capable of either, or had been once. There was a time in his life when it would have meant nothing to him.

He wasn't the person he had been, but he believed he could do what was necessary if it came to that. He didn't want to do it, but he also didn't want the man alive. As long as that private detective was breathing Harry knew he was in danger. He asked himself if he could live with that knowledge and, after some time, decided he could.

For now.

It would be best to simply pay the man. Probably that would be enough – almost certainly that would be enough – and he could live with the small chance that it wasn't. He thought he could. There would be times when the knowledge wormed its way into his brain. There would be times when he'd be able to think of little else. He knew that. He knew how his mind worked. But living with that would be better than killing again. He didn't want to become the person he had once been. He hated that person.

He also feared him.

He might be chained to the man, but that did not mean they must become one. He was a prisoner shackled to a criminal worse than himself, but that man's crimes did not have to be his. Particularly since the man he was shackled to was dead. It was weight he was dragging, and that was all.

The person he had been was responsible for his losing everything he'd ever loved – his wife and his son – and he now had a chance to get his son back.

Harry White had that chance.

Harry Combs was dead, and he needed to *stay* dead.

He might have to drag him along for the rest of his life, but he'd done it now for twenty-six years. He could live with that.

'I don't trust him.'

Harry jumped at the sound of Teresa's voice. He'd thought she was asleep – usually she fell into a drunken sleep the moment her head hit the pillow – but when he glanced over at her he saw that she was staring thoughtfully at the ceiling.

'What?'

She squeezed his hand and looked toward him. Her eyes were watery and red, but she appeared to be sober or close to it. There was sharpness to her look that he hadn't seen in a very long time; there was bright awareness there. Her eyes almost seemed to glow in the dark room, brighter somehow than anything else.

'I don't trust him.'

'Who?'

'Andrew.'

'What do you mean?'

'I know he's your son, and I think I have some idea how you feel about what happened. I want to be happy he's here. But – but I'm *not*. I don't trust him. I don't like him and I don't trust him and I wish he'd never shown up here.'

Harry blinked. He didn't know what to say. He didn't know what to think.

Part of him hated Teresa for saying what she said, for what she said was an echo of thoughts he'd pushed to the back of his own mind.

'Don't talk like that, Teresa.'

'How should I talk, Harry?'

'Not like that.'

'After all these years, you want me to lie to you?'

'No.'

'Then what?'

Harry didn't answer for a long time, then he said: 'I want you to feel differently.'

'But I don't.'

'Can you try?'

'I *want* to feel differently, Harry, but there's something about him that's – there's something about him that feels *wrong*.'

Harry knew what Teresa had picked up on. There was rage in Andrew's eyes, and there was hatred as well. But both of those things were understandable. They didn't mean that anything was wrong with the boy. They meant only that he was human, and that he needed time.

He needed time.

THEN:

Paul Watkins begins to thumb back the hammer but, not ready to die, Harry lunges at him with the knife.

Watkins steps aside, the blade cutting only air. Harry slams into him and both of them fall to the asphalt, a grunt escaping Watkins as the air is pounded from his lungs. The gun falls from the man's hand and rattles against the ground.

Harry pushes himself up and lifts his arm. It hangs over Watkins's face a moment, and then Harry drops it down, knife gripped in his fist.

Watkins grabs Harry's wrist before the blade makes contact.

Harry leans into it, putting his weight down.

Watkins's arms begin to shake, and then they give, but he manages to roll out from under Harry just in time.

The knife hits asphalt and the blade snaps in two.

Harry tosses the handle away, looking for another weapon.

A cinderblock rests amongst a pile of construction waste.

Harry goes for it, but before he can take even two full steps

Watkins grabs his ankle and pulls it out from under him. Harry falls down face-forward and the ground rushes up at him, a gray blur. The asphalt cuts into his palms as he reaches out to catch himself.

Then he continues to crawl for the cinderblock.

He grabs it with both hands and turns over just in time to see Watkins coming for him. As Watkins falls upon him, revolver thankfully forgotten for the moment, Harry swings the cinderblock up with both hands, smashing it into his face. The nose snaps and blood pours down over his mouth.

Watkins steps back once, twice, and then falls to a sitting position, looking dazed.

Harry gets to his feet, cinderblock gripped in both hands, and walks toward him.

NOW:

1

Andrew awakened the next morning from a nightmare. He was overwhelmed briefly by a deep sadness. It was, for a time, the only thing he felt or was capable of feeling. Then, slowly, it faded away, like the night itself, leaving him empty. Here he was under the same roof as his father yet he still did not know what came next. He had believed that once faced with his father things would come into focus. He'd believed he would know what to do once he looked into the man's eyes. Instead he felt as lost as ever.

The situation was a blur and no matter what direction he turned he could not find focus.

He pushed himself to the edge of the bed and sat up, feet on the floor. He looked at the wall across from him. It was white. He looked at the framed oil painting which hung there. It told him nothing. It could have been hanging in any hotel room in America.

He looked down at his pale bare legs and felt very vulnerable.

His pants lay in a pile on the floor. He got to his feet, picked them up, and slipped into them. He put on a T-shirt. Tiny holes dotted the front of it, evidence of his using the shirt to twist off beer caps. He looked toward the bedroom door. It was closed. He imagined opening it and finding himself in a different world. He imagined opening it and—

He pulls the door open and finds himself in Dallas, Texas, 1964. This is the house he once lived in when he was a baby, when both his parents were still alive. He stands in a foyer, a hat tree to his right with a single fedora hanging from a hand-carved branch. The living room sits before him. And to his left, the hallway.

He turns left and heads down the hallway.

At the other end of it his father stands in a doorway. He has his back to Andrew. He's looking in at a room, at the goings-on within the room.

Andrew can hear the sound of panicked voices. The voices belong to his mother and Paul Watkins. He's heard them dozens of times in his memories, and has always been certain of them, but somehow today he is not. And though he's never before understood what they were saying, he understands what they're saying now. He understands because he is no longer a baby. He is a man.

'Hurry it up, Helen,' Paul Watkins says, 'we don't have much time.'

'I'm packing as fast as I can, Paul.'

The man in the doorway – his father – raises the revolver in his hand.

A sudden weight brings down Andrew's own hand. He looks at it and sees a pistol hanging there. Of course: he knows what to do. He knows what to do and he must do it quickly. If he doesn't do it quickly it will be too late.

He raises the pistol in his hand and aims it at the back of his father's head, the gun shaking, shaking, shaking, and he tries to steady himself, tries to build up the determination to do this thing, to do what he has to do, goddamn it – just do it, you fucking coward – but before he can squeeze the trigger, if he was in fact going to do it, of which he cannot be certain, his father squeezes his.

Something thuds to the floor like a sack of potatoes.

His mother begins screaming.

His father's gun goes off again and the screaming stops.

Now only the baby in that room emits sound – the eighteen-month-old him. He cries loudly and without restraint.

After an empty moment, his father turns around and looks at him, looks him in the eye. For a moment – less than a second – the face is not the one he expects. For a moment he is looking at Paul Watkins, and the man on the floor behind him, lying on his side and bleeding from a wound in his head, is Harry Combs. Then the figures shift, it takes only the blink of an eye, and he is looking at Harry Combs.

They are both young men, within a decade of one another in age. They could easily be mistaken for brothers.

His father frowns. For he is certain that Harry Combs is, in fact, his father. In his heart he's certain of it. He could not have this much hate for anyone to whom he were not tied by blood, for familial hate is the strongest hate there is, and his could be no stronger.

'I knew you wouldn't be able to do it.'

His father raises the revolver, points it at Andrew's face.

Andrew imagines that he can see down its long barrel to the spent shell at the other end – what is left of the round that killed his mother.

His father thumbs back the hammer and the cylinder rotates. A new round comes into view. Hello, non-existence, it's been a while.

'You get one more chance,' his father says. 'You get to the count of three. One.'

Andrew can see in his father's eyes that he means it. There is but a single way that he will walk breathing from this situation: if his father does not. He raises the pistol in his own shaking hand. It feels heavy there. It feels like it weighs a ton. It must be the densest metal on earth. It's difficult even to keep it raised.

'Two.'

His face balls up with emotion. The gun shakes harder. He tells himself to do it, just fucking do *it, Andrew, you goddamn piece of shit, you stupid motherfucker.*

'Three.'

His father squeezes the trigger.

Andrew walked to the door and pulled it open. He found himself just where he should have found himself, just *when* he should have found himself.

He walked to the kitchen. His father stood at the stove making scrambled eggs in one pan while sausages fried in another. His father was the old man he should have been, wearing a tattered cardigan over his slumped shoulders, face emotionless as he cooked.

Teresa was sitting at the kitchen table in a bathrobe. She poured herself a drink from a new bottle of vodka – she must have had several of them in the freezer – and brought it to her lips with a shaking right hand.

Toast popped from the toaster. Andrew jumped at the sound, and a small yelp escaped his throat before he could think to repress it.

His father looked over at him and smiled.

'Morning.'

Andrew nodded.

'Mind buttering the toast before it gets cold?'

'Okay.' He walked toward the toaster.

2

Harry walked upstairs to his library and simply stood there for a very long time before making his way to the safe and unlocking it. Every time he did this it felt as though he was unlocking the past, and the past was a sad place. It hurt to visit, and though part of him liked the hurt, or had liked the hurt – as recently as the day before yesterday – he didn't want to visit it now. He wanted only to be in the present with his son, with his second chance.

He reached into the safe and removed a ten-thousand-dollar bundle of hundred-dollar bills. He thumbed through the money. This was his payment for getting his son back, and when he thought of it like that it didn't seem much payment at all. He slipped it into the pocket of his khaki pants. He shut the safe, hoping that doing so would shut off the past as well, but enough of it had escaped already to affect his mood.

It was hard to shut off the past when you were still dealing with it.

He walked back downstairs. Andrew was sitting on the couch in the living room.

'You ready to head out?'

Andrew nodded and got to his feet.

When he glanced out his storefront window at half past eight he saw the private detective's Honda Prelude parked at the curb. A sigh escaped him. He knew it would be there but despite this his stomach went sour upon seeing it. The greasy son of a bitch raised a hand in greeting. Harry – feeling childish – gave him the finger and turned away.

Looking toward the back of his store he watched Andrew shelving books. This morning over breakfast Harry had mentioned to Teresa that he was planning on hiring someone to work part-time in the shop and Andrew volunteered to work for him while he was in town. He said he lived with a girl back home and bills were tight even when they were both employed full-time.

It was the first time he'd told Harry anything personal about himself. He had a girl back home. It filled him with joy and made him sad simultaneously. His son was a man and had a life with a young lady, and these were good things. But the fact that he was only learning about them made him realize how much he'd missed. His son was twenty-seven years old, and for years he'd had fantasies of their being reunited, but his fantasies had been so empty. They were only ideas. He'd not been able to fill in the details, for he knew none of the details. He hadn't even realized their absence until he was presented with one of them, and that one seemed to represent hundreds of others he didn't know. What did Andrew's apartment look like? What did his neighborhood look like? Where did he take his girl to dinner on special occasions? The questions were infinite, or nearly so.

A knock at the front door caused Harry to turn around.

The private detective stood on the other side of the glass.

Harry shook his head and pointed at his watch.

'You've gotta be kidding me.'

Harry shook his head again. He was going to have to deal with the guy soon, but right now was not soon. He wondered what Andrew would think of the exchange – if he witnessed it. He wondered if Ãndrew knew what this private detective looked like. He hoped that he didn't, hoped their interactions had been long-distance only, as he didn't want his son to know the trouble he'd caused.

The private detective pushed his way through the door. He was wearing a green and burgundy striped shirt with the open collar revealing a gold chain around his neck, dark jeans, and brown boots with square toes. His shirt was tucked into his jeans and he was wearing a thin braided belt.

He smiled as he turned toward Harry and said: 'Beautiful morning, yeah?'

'I'm in no mood for small talk.'

The private detective shrugged. 'No skin off my nose. Let's get this done.'

Harry shook his head. 'I want to know exactly who you are.'

'We been over this.'

'No, we've only discussed *what* you are. I'd like to know who you are.'

The man removed a brown leather wallet and opened it. He pulled from within a cheaply printed white business card held between index and middle finger and swept the card toward Harry with a flourish. Harry took it and gave it a look. The man's name was Silas Green, and he had an office on Preston Highway, down near the airport, the top-less bars, and the seedy motels.

The first time Silas Green walked in here Harry had been in shock, having just learned that there was a man in the world with knowledge that could destroy his life, but that information had since sunk in, so when he looked up from the man's amateurish business card this morning and peered at him he was able to see him for what he was rather than seeing him merely as a threat. He looked at the pockmarked face. He looked at the uncared-for fingernails. He looked at the flashy but cheap jewelry. He looked at the expensive but ancient shoes, scuffed and badly in need of replacement. And he looked at the crooked but toothy grin, like his jewelry all flash with no substance.

The man was a punk.

It was as simple as that. He was a goddamn *punk*. And there was a part of him that bristled at being taken by a punk, by the kind of man Harry Combs would have chewed up and spit out in a matter of seconds. If Silas Green were a real man this would be easier. It wouldn't be *easy* – it's never easy to take a push and not push back – but he'd not feel the same tightness in his chest, the same urge to bash this man's face against the counter till it was pulp and bone shards. As it was he could hardly stomach it.

Silas Green must have sensed Harry's state of mind, too, for the grin fell from his cunt mouth and some of the confidence left him.

'Is – is there a problem?'

Harry shook his head, his lips tight, his eyes locked on the man standing across from him. 'No,' he said, removing the ten thousand dollars from his right hip pocket. He set the bundle on the counter. 'But if I ever see you again there will be.'

Silas Green reached out to take the money but Harry stopped him by grabbing his wrist in his hand. He clenched it till he saw pain contort Silas Green's face.

'Are we clear on that?'

'Let go my hand.'

'Are we clear?'

Silas Green nodded.

'I want you to say it.'

'We're clear, man, now let go my hand.'

Harry loosened his grip and Silas Green pulled away. He grabbed the money, pocketed it, then rubbed at his wrist.

He smiled once more, though there was less flash in it than before, less confidence. 'I won't say it's been a pleasure.'

'Get the fuck out of my store.'

3

Andrew watched the front desk from the back of the store, a pile of books in his arms. He watched as his father set down a large stack of money. He watched as the man standing across from him reached for it. He watched as his father grabbed the man's wrist and spoke to him through an angry mouth. The look in his eyes was intense and cold.

It changed him.

This was the man Andrew had expected to encounter: this angry man capable of snapping a neck without remorse.

After another exchange of words the man turned and walked out through the door. He paused at the curb, waited for traffic to clear, and made his way across the street. His father watched him through the window, watched him until he started his car, pulled out into the street, and disappeared from view.

Then he turned back to face his store.

His eyes locked on Andrew's and when they did Andrew saw something new in his face. He didn't think it was fear but he thought it was something related to fear. Andrew had seen something his father hadn't wanted him to see. He wished he knew what it was. He wished he understood the context of what he had witnessed.

'What was that about?'

His father was silent for a long time before saying: 'Business.'

'It didn't look like business.'

'It was unpleasant business.'

'What was it about?'

His father again went silent. He seemed to be having

an internal debate of some kind. His eyes went thoughtful and his face shifted with his emotional reactions to various considerations, or perhaps to their consequences. Finally he looked again at Andrew and said: 'He knows who I am, who I used to be.'

'How did – how did he find out?'

'He's a private detective.'

With those words Andrew understood. He was the reason the man had walked in here. He was the reason his father'd had to hand over a stack of money. His search for the man had also brought others to his door. His search had brought bad men to his door – one bad man anyway, a man who believed he was a wolf.

Harry Combs would have killed that private detective. Of that Andrew was certain. Harry Combs would have killed him without a second thought. Harry White had simply paid him. There might have been a flash of Harry Combs in his eyes, but his actions were all Harry White. So perhaps his father wasn't the man he once had been. Perhaps he really *had* changed. Perhaps this rage he felt was for a man who was dead, for a man who'd been dead more than a quarter-century. If that was true he needed to find a way to release it, for there was no point in directing anger and hatred at the dead. Hatred in particular was a corrosive emotion; it rusted the soul. If left to work long enough it would destroy the soul, eat it away until there was nothing left, nothing worth saving anyway.

But looking at his father he did not believe that Harry

Combs was dead. He was in there somewhere. He was in there but buried.

Andrew wanted to bring him out. He wanted to see that man living and breathing in the real world rather than only in his mind. If he could see his father as he knew he really was – as he really had been – then he could do what he believed he had to do.

Then he might not feel the weight of all this.

He felt heavy with excess: excess organs, excess thoughts, excess skin, excess eyes, excess teeth. He was two people at once and he needed to cut one of them away. He needed to cut Harry Combs away. But the only way he could justify to himself what he wanted to do was to prove that Harry Combs was actually still alive somewhere, for you could not kill the dead.

He didn't know how he was going to prove that to himself, but he knew that he had to. That lack of certainty was what had been holding him back. It had kept him confused and lost. He needed to find Harry Combs so that he could cut him away, and in cutting him away become himself. It was as simple and as complicated as that.

'Andrew?'

He looked up at his father.

'You okay?'

He nodded. 'I am.'

And he was. He was more okay than he'd been in a long time.

Finally he knew what he needed to do. Finally he

knew how to move forward rather than backward. Finally he knew consciously what he had known in those shadowed corners of his mind all along.

He had to kill his father.

But first he had to prove to himself that his father was still alive, and he didn't know how he might do that. He thought he could see Harry Combs poking through the facade every now and then, but that wasn't enough. He needed to see the man brought fully to life, like a golem – he needed to see him brought fully to life in order that he might kill him.

How he was going to make that happen he did not know.

The techniques employed will vary according to whether the subject is unaware of his danger, aware but unguarded, or guarded. They will also be affected by whether or not the assassin is to be killed with the subject. Hereafter, assassinations in which the subject is unaware will be termed 'simple'; those where the subject is aware but unguarded will be termed 'chase'; those where the victim is guarded will be termed 'guarded'.

If the assassin is to die with the subject, the act will be called 'lost'. If the assassin is to escape, the adjective will be 'safe'. It should be noted that no compromises should exist here. The assassin must not fall alive into enemy hands.

A further type division is caused by the need to conceal the fact that the subject was actually the victim of assassination, rather than an accident or natural causes. If such concealment is desirable the operation will be called 'secret'; if concealment is immaterial, the act will be called 'open'; while if the assassination requires publicity to be effective it will be termed 'terroristic'.

Following these definitions, the assassination of Julius Caesar was safe, simple, and terroristic, while that of Huey Long was lost, guarded and open.

Obviously, successful secret assassinations are not recorded as assassination at all. Augustus Caesar may have been the victim of a safe, guarded and secret assassination.

Chase assassinations usually involve clandestine agents or members of criminal organizations.

In safe assassinations, the assassin needs the usual qualities of a clandestine agent. He should be determined, courageous, intelligent, resourceful, and physically active. If special equipment is to be used, such as firearms or drugs, it is clear that he must have outstanding skill with such equipment.

Except in terroristic assassinations, it is desirable that the assassin be transient in the area. He should have an absolute minimum of contact with the rest of the organization and his instructions should be given orally by one person only. His safe evacuation after the act is absolutely essential, but here again contact should be as limited as possible. It is preferable that the person issuing instructions also conduct any withdrawal or covering action which may be necessary.

In lost assassination, the assassin must be a fanatic of some sort. Politics, religion, and revenge are about the only feasible motives. Since a fanatic is unstable psychologically, he must be handled with extreme care. He must not know the identities of the other members of the organization, for although it is intended that he die in the act, something may go wrong. While the assassin of Trotsky has never revealed any significant information, it was unsound to depend on this when the act was planned.

When the decision to assassinate has been reached, the tactics of the operation must be planned, based upon an estimate of the situation similar to that used in military operations. The preliminary estimate will reveal gaps in information and possibly indicate a need for special equipment which must be procured or constructed. When all necessary data has been collected, an effective tactical plan can be prepared. All planning must be mental; no papers should ever contain evidence of the operation.

In resistance situations, assassination may be used as a counter-reprisal. Since this requires advertising to be effective, the resistance organization must be in a position to warn high officials publicly that their lives will be the price of reprisal action against innocent people. Such a threat is of no value unless it can be carried out, so it may be necessary to plan the assassination of various responsible officers of the oppressive regime and hold such plans in readiness to be used only if provoked by excessive brutality. Such plans must be modified frequently to meet changes in the tactical situation.

The essential point of assassination is the death of the

subject. A human being may be killed in many ways but sureness is often overlooked by those who may be emotionally unstrung by the seriousness of this act they intend to commit. The specific technique employed will depend upon a large number of variables, but should be constant in one point: Death must be absolutely certain. The attempt on Hitler's life failed because the conspiracy did not give this matter proper attention.

PART TWO

MINUS

In nature there are neither rewards nor punishments – there are consequences.
Robert G. Ingersoll

THEN:

Harry throws three dollars down on the table and gets to his feet. He walks to the back of the diner, where a payphone hangs on the wall. He picks it up. He dials an operator. He speaks to her, and then drops half a dozen coins into the machine. After several clicks, he hears a ringing in his ear. Then a woman's voice: 'Hello?'

'It's me.'

A long pause, and then: 'What's going on, Harry?'

'Is Andrew there?'

'A woman came by with him yesterday.'

'She didn't explain the situation to you?'

'I didn't understand what she was talking about.'

'Helen's dead and he isn't safe with me.'

Another silence.

'Mom?'

'I can't believe this,' she says. 'I can't believe how you always mess everything up.'

Years ago she would have reacted in a very different way. She would have been shocked. She would have said, what? How can this be? How can this be? There would already have been tears. After the tears would have come the recrimination. But it isn't years ago – it's now – so she skips the first part and moves directly to telling Harry how useless he is.

Harry closes his eyes and resists the urge to snap at his mother. His entire life she has told him he's a piece of shit in one way or another and somehow she expects him to be something else. He doesn't understand how he could have been. You're useless. You're nothing. You're a waste of breath – a waste of life. Sometimes I wish you'd been stillborn.

'How did you turn out this way?'

With his eyes still closed: 'I'm sorry.'

His mother begins to cry. 'I don't know what sorry is supposed to do.'

He opens his eyes. 'I was just calling to make sure he arrived safely. Goodbye.'

He hangs up the phone and looks at it in silence for a long time. Then he turns and walks back through the diner toward the front door.

'See you later, hon,' his waitress says.

'I doubt it.'

He pushes out into the sunshine. It's time for him to leave Texas. He's only an hour from the border, so it will be happening soon. It's time for him to leave and never return.

After pulling open his car door he falls into the leather seat. He turns the key in the ignition and the car rumbles to life. He puts the car into gear and pulls out of the parking lot. He makes a left onto the street and heads toward the interstate.

He gives everything he's ever known a silent goodbye.

It's all in his rearview mirror now.

NOW:

1

Nothing much happened until the following Monday. The days merely went as days go, one after the other the same as the one before. A few small things occurred, but they were barely worth mentioning. Andrew worked in his father's bookshop, ate at his father's table, slept in his father's guest bedroom. He called Melissa twice and told her what was happening, though he neglected to reveal what was going on internally. She responded coolly. When his father paid him in cash on Friday he sent her the money. He watched his father closely, hoping to see Harry Combs inside him somewhere. He wondered how to bring him out, but didn't know how, and the man did not reveal himself.

Then, on Monday, the private detective returned.

That changed everything.

2

Harry was standing behind the counter ringing up Bukowski's *Women* for a young man in a grease-stained T-shirt when Silas Green pushed his way through the door. At first glance Harry didn't recognize him – he'd not expected to see him again, not in his store, and so had filed his face away in the back drawers of his mind – but when upon his second glance he realized who it was his stomach went sour and his lips began to tingle.

This man was going to be trouble. He was too stupid to realize when he'd pushed someone as far as that someone *could* be pushed. He didn't understand that when you pushed a man too far he would spring back and knock you down, not because he wanted to but because that was the nature of things. It was downright Newtonian. Harry had been close to that point already. Now he was there. He didn't even need to hear what the son of a bitch had to say; his mere presence in the store pushed him to that point.

Harry tore the receipt from his register, tucked it into the book and said: 'Enjoy. Not his best work, bit repetitive, but it does have its moments. Next time grab *Post Office* or *Ham on Rye* if you haven't read them yet.'

The young man made brief eye contact, dropped his gaze, and headed out the door in silence, watching his feet kick out one in front of the other.

Harry looked toward Silas Green. 'What the fuck are you doing here?'

Silas Green looked at him with bloodshot eyes and for a time said nothing. He cleared his throat. He looked down at his shoes. He looked back up. There was a yellowing crescent bruise lining his left eye socket. The man had had a busy weekend.

Finally he spoke. 'I need money.'

'Then you'd better get to work.'

'I need a lot of money.'

'Then you'd better work hard.'

The man said nothing.

'I gave you all the money I'm going to.'

'But it's gone – it's gone and I'm upside down with people I can't afford to be upside down with.'

'I don't care.'

'You – you *should*. With what I know about you you should care.'

'I paid you once for your silence. I won't pay twice for the same thing.'

'I don't see as you have much of a choice.'

Harry smiled, though he knew there was no humor in it. 'The way I see it, I have a very clear choice – a *very* clear choice – and I'm not leaning toward paying you.'

'I need the money. I'll pay you back.'

'You want to borrow money from me to pay back someone you borrowed money from, and I'm supposed to believe you'll pay *me* back? You gonna borrow that from a third party? You're running your life like a Ponzi scheme, and that's no way to run a life. I've been alive a bit longer than you, so let me tell you something you might not already know: a man never gets out of a hole by digging his way down. You won't come out the other side, son. It simply won't happen. In the history of the world it never has yet.'

'I don't need advice. I need money.'

'You're not getting it here.'

Anger flashed in Silas Green's eyes and he pounded the counter with the flat of his palm. 'God*damn* it. I can destroy your fucking life. You'll give me the money, and I'm not gonna pay you back a fucking dime, and if you *don't* give me the money I'll see to it that you spend the rest of your miserable life rotting away in prison, and that's if you're lucky. I might just get in touch with some former associates of yours in Dallas. See if I won't, pal.'

'I tried to do this your way. That was a mistake. So now we do this *my* way. You get the fuck out of my store. Get out now. And know this: you've just killed yourself. You've just committed suicide. If you're walking down the street and you hear a noise behind you, it's probably me. Because I'm coming for you, you dumb son of a bitch. I'll wait for my moment and I'll take it. You won't live long enough to say word one to the cops – or to anyone else. You're a fucking dead man.'

For a moment Silas Green looked genuinely scared, but

managed either to think himself out of it or to push the fear to the back of his mind.

'We both know that's bluster,' he said.

Without warning or indication Harry grabbed the letter opener from his counter and swiped it quickly at Silas Green's face. His cheek opened up to reveal the red meat within. After a moment blood began to flow. And the whole time Silas Green simply stood there, arms at his sides. He seemed to not even know what had happened.

Harry pulled a Kleenex from the box on his counter, wiped the blade of his letter opener, and tossed the tissue into his trash can.

When he looked back up to Silas Green the man was touching his cheek. His eyes were wide. It had finally registered in his slow brain.

'Tell me again it's bluster,' Harry said. He grabbed another Kleenex and handed it to Silas Green. 'You're bleeding on my floor.'

Silas Green took the Kleenex and put it to his cheek. 'Thank you,' he said. His eyes remained wide with shock, his voice sounded distant. The Kleenex filled with blood almost immediately. He simply stood there holding it.

'I'd kill you now if I didn't know better. But I *do* know better. I know better than to kill a man in my own store. I know better than to kill while filled with as much anger as I'm now filled with. But you're a dead man all the same. Now get the fuck out of my store before I lose my shit and do you right here despite my knowing better.'

Silas Green nodded. He turned away, took two steps, turned back.

'I'm – I'm sorry. I was desperate.'

'It's too late for that. I know what kind of man you are now, and I can't trust you with information.'

'I understand.'

Silas Green walked out of the bookshop.

Harry sat down. He put his head in his hands. He exhaled. During the confrontation he felt fine, or perhaps he was unaware of everything he felt, but now he was shaky and emotionally drained. He'd not had such a confrontation in many years. He'd not let that side of him out in many years. Now he was in the strange position of needing that side of himself in order to protect his other self, and he didn't want to let it out. He knew it was in there – he'd known all along that it was in there – but he'd thought himself incapable of going there without intentionally willing himself to go there. He'd thought Harry White had such dominance over his behavior that Harry Combs would never be able to escape on his own. He knew now that that was untrue. Harry Combs had simply been waiting for his moment, and he'd taken it, and if it happened again he might never be able to push him back down into the cave in which he'd been hibernating for the last two and a half decades.

Harry Combs was patient, but he was also strong.

'Are you really going to kill him?'

Harry looked up.

Andrew stood on the other side of the counter looking back. His expression was flat. His eyes were dull.

Harry didn't know how to answer, in part because he didn't know what the answer was. He hadn't thought about whether or not he would follow through; he'd simply tried to frighten the man with his threat.

But the question was an important one.

3

The private detective walked out of the store. The door swung shut behind him. His father watched this, as did Andrew, then sat down and put his head in his hands. Andrew walked toward him slowly. He didn't know what to think, what to feel.

He'd seen Harry Combs unleashed for the first time since his arrival in Louisville. Yes, he'd seen a flash of him before – but this was his first time seeing the man in action – and it was a strange experience. His father's eyes actually seemed to change color. They seemed to go darker. His soft face went hard and stony. His mouth changed.

He'd never seen such a transformation before, and though he'd known this other man was living within the kind, gentle bookseller he'd begun to feel he knew, the change had been disconcerting. There'd been something almost supernatural about it – something *unnatural*, anyway.

He stopped at the counter and looked at his father.

'Are you really going to kill him?'

His father looked up. The bastard was gone from him, the kind old bookseller taking up residence once more.

'I don't know,' he said after a while. 'I don't think so.'

'Then what will you do?'

'Nothing. I think scaring him was enough.'

'But you don't know that.'

'I don't.'

'Then how can you leave it like this?'

'I don't see that I have an option.'

'You could – you could do what you threatened to do.'

His father looked at him for a long time. Andrew could not read his expression, nor could he read his eyes, but something was happening within him.

Finally his father said: 'I don't want you to think that way. I don't want you to be like me – like I used to be.'

'But I think you should. You're not safe if he's alive. I brought this to your door and I don't want to see you ruined by it. I couldn't live with myself.'

4

Andrew was right. Harry wasn't sure he trusted his son's motives – there was something about the boy's tone he did not like – but he knew he should kill Silas Green, had known it might come to that from the beginning, but did not want to face that fact. For he did not want to become the man he'd once been. It felt somehow contradictory to become that person in order to protect the man he now was. Like whoring out your wife in order to keep the finances in order and avoid divorce. But he knew he might lose himself completely if he didn't. He would be extradited, tried, and – Texas being what it was – very possibly put to death. And that was if Rathbone didn't get to him first.

And what would become of Teresa if that happened?

Very likely she'd drink herself to death in a matter of months.

He knew she was drinking herself to death now, and he knew too that he was allowing it to happen – she'd already been hospitalized twice – but she was doing it at a reasonable pace. There was still a chance that she might turn it around. He thought it unlikely, but unlikely was better than the alternative.

And what would become of his relationship with his son?

It would be dead before it had even fairly been birthed. It would simply be finished.

'You're right,' he said. 'I have to do it.'

5

'I want to help.'

He spoke those four words without fully considering them. Yet they were true. He wanted to be a part of it. He needed to be a part of it. It was his reason for pushing his father toward assassination in the first place. Here was this man he had no feelings for whatsoever. Here he was practically *trying* to get himself killed, for only a suicidal man would threaten someone he knew was fully capable of murder, and here was Andrew with a need to prove to himself that he was capable of it. If he was going to take care of his father – a man for whom he held complex and contradictory emotions – he needed to know he could do it by taking care of a man, by at least helping to take care of a man, for whom he felt nothing.

And he needed his father to teach him how these things were done. He was twenty-seven years old and, aside from a few fist fights, a few acts of angry vandalism, had spent most of those years on the right side of the law. Violence was something he felt in his heart, felt strongly in his heart, but did not act upon. He needed his father to guide him, to teach him how such things were done – for if his father knew anything it was murder – but he would never do such a thing if he knew Andrew's ultimate goal.

The private detective masked that goal.

So yes – he wanted to help. He *needed* to help.

His father shook his head. 'No,' he said. 'We shouldn't be talking about this at all. I'll do what I have to do, but I don't want us to discuss this – not now, not ever.'

'I started this,' Andrew said. 'I want to help finish it.'

'I'm not getting you involved in this.'

'I *am* involved. It's only happening because of me.'

Andrew wondered if he would really be able to take this all the way. He wondered if he really had it in him. He believed he did.

But if he let it out would that mean he was as bad as his father? Was he actually becoming more like this man he hated in order that he might destroy him, and in destroying the man outside himself would he be reborn within him? Or was he different because the man he wanted dead actually *deserved* to die?

But what about the private detective? Was he willing to kill a man just to be certain he was capable of doing to his father what needed to be done, just to learn how in fact it *was* done? He didn't know. He wished he did, but he didn't.

All he knew for certain was what he felt, and he felt he needed to do this.

If he could take the life of this stranger, if his father could teach him the family trade, then he might actually be able to follow through on his real task. By taking the life of the man who taught him to kill.

He'd worry about what that meant later. Sometimes there was no logic to what the heart needed.

His father sighed: 'Maybe you should head back to California.'

'What?'

'I'd hate to see you go so soon, but I don't want you involved in this.'

'I already told you, I *am* involved. If you don't let me be part of this, part of the solution, you'll never see me again. I can promise you that. If you send me away now, you'll never fucking see me again. Not in a year, not in *twenty* years.'

6

Harry was silent for a long time. He didn't know what to say, what to do. The thought of losing his son again so soon after getting him back was devastating. But he also didn't want Andrew to become what he had been, and he was afraid that would happen. He was almost certain that would happen. And yet – and yet: there was a chance it would not. Perhaps Andrew wanted this only so he could understand fully who Harry Combs had been, and didn't he deserve that? Didn't he deserve answers?

He did, and this was really the only way he'd ever get them.

After a long time Harry finally spoke. 'Okay,' he said.

'Okay,' Andrew said. 'Good.'

THEN:

He isn't sure why he stops in Louisville. Perhaps simply because it's a place he's never once given a single thought to. Perhaps because it has nothing to do with him at all. He might have gone to New York or Los Angeles or Chicago. He might have gone to any number of large cities in which he could easily disappear. But each of those cities already exists in his mind and has for years. Louisville is a blank slate – it might be anything – and he thinks that is exactly what he needs: a blank slate on which he can write his new life, his new self.

So when he reaches Louisville he stops.

He eats frog legs at a seafood restaurant on the Ohio River, and afterwards he stands outside and looks across the water and decides to stay.

He might as well. He belongs nowhere else. Hell, he hasn't even been born yet – the person he is to become hasn't – and as far as he can tell this is as good a birthplace as any.

'Welcome home,' he says aloud as a breeze blows across the river and ruffles his hair. 'Welcome home, Harry White.'

NOW:

1

Andrew sat in the passenger seat while his father drove the car south on Preston Highway. It was just past eight o'clock in the morning and they'd already made two stops. They went to the bookshop to put up a sign that informed potential customers the place was closed due to illness and also stopped at a small house in Germantown, a property Teresa owned and usually rented out. The last tenants were evicted a couple weeks ago and his father wanted to make certain they were actually out; otherwise he'd have to call the sheriff.

Andrew didn't know why he'd do that today, do that in the middle of doing what they were doing today, but he had.

The air was fairly cool still from several hours of night, but it was at the cusp of uncomfortable and would be downright hot in another hour, and barely tolerable an hour after that, the sky clear of clouds and the sun burning white-hot above them.

His father sat silent beside him, had been silent since they left Germantown, hands gripping the steering wheel, and when Andrew turned on the radio – halfway through 'Play With Fire' by the Rolling Stones – his father without a word reached down and turned it off again.

And so the silence continued.

It continued while they drove along with traffic past the theme park, past the airport, past Godfather's, and past several massage parlors with blacked-out windows before finally arriving at a run-down strip mall which was home to three vacant storefronts, a fried chicken restaurant, a VHS rental place, and Silas Green Investigations.

It continued while his father drove past the strip mall – giving it barely a glance – and at the next light flipped a horseshoe.

It continued while he drove back a block and pulled into a diner parking lot.

It continued as he stepped from the vehicle.

After a moment Andrew stepped out as well.

He looked toward his father.

His father was squinting across traffic to the strip mall, to Silas Green Investigations.

The man's car was absent and there were no lights on behind the windows. Except for vinyl lettering on the glass the place looked as disused as the vacant space next door.

'I haven't smoked a cigarette in decades,' his father said, 'but I'd kill for one right now.'

After a moment he chuckled at himself, at his turn of phrase, but there didn't seem to be any humor in it.

Following another long silence during which his father only continued to stare across the street Andrew said: 'What now?'

His father glanced toward him. 'We get some breakfast.'

'I'm not hungry.'

'That's fine,' his father said. 'Food is secondary.'

2

Harry walked into the diner. Andrew followed behind him. The place had a fly-spotted acoustic ceiling and wood-paneled walls, which made Harry feel as though he were walking into a badly finished basement. A few other customers were scattered about at random tables, folks in stained T-shirts and John Deere or U of L baseball caps, in cargo shorts or faded Levi's. They sat and talked and ate chicken fried steak and eggs, waffles, stacks of pancakes. They sipped coffee and orange juice. Cigarettes sat in ashtrays on tables, smoke wafting toward the ceiling.

Harry and Andrew stepped to a sign which said PLEASE WAIT TO BE SEATED and a moment later were greeted by a heavy-set blonde woman in a pink dress. She smiled at them – a wad of stinking green bubblegum pinched between her large horse teeth – and asked is it just the two of you then?

'That's right.'

She grabbed a couple laminated menus. 'Follow me.'

'I'd like to sit at that table if it's all right.' Harry pointed toward a four-top set up before the fingerprinted front window.

'I don't see why not.'

'Thank you.'

Harry and Andrew sat down at a scratched Formica table. The hostess set the plastic-lined menus in front of them. Harry's was dotted with what he thought was gravy of some sort. He scanned the menu and thought about the fact that he hadn't prepared anything for Teresa this morning. She'd probably be in a worse state than usual when he arrived home this evening. He wished he'd taken the time, but it simply hadn't been there to take. There were other things he needed to do today.

He looked out the window.

'How involved in this do you want to be?'

After a long time Andrew finally answered: 'I wanna pull the trigger.'

Harry nodded to himself. He'd thought Andrew would say that. Were he in Andrew's position he'd have said the same thing – were he both that naive and that angry – but time has a way of sucking that sort of foolhardy gutsiness out of a man. Little children and those nearing or beyond retirement age: they both know that sometimes darkness really does have monsters in it. Maybe because they're so much closer to darkness than those in early adulthood. Children have just crawled out of it, after all, and those who have crested life's mountain and are heading down the other side know they will soon be crawling back into it: that low, eternal night which hovers there like a black fog. You must be old enough to have forgotten the swirling vacuum of pre-existence and young enough to believe you will never die in order to be fearless in that way.

'I don't think it will be as easy as you suppose,' he said.

'I don't think it *will* be easy.'

'Why do you want to do it?'

'I created this problem. I wanna be the solution.'

Harry turned and looked at his son. His son looked back, his gaze unwavering.

'There's more to it than that, isn't there?'

Andrew dropped his head, looked down at the menu. After some time: 'I want to know what it *feels* like.'

'If you put yourself in the right frame of mind it doesn't feel like anything.'

'I don't understand.'

'I know,' Harry said.

'So explain it to me.'

'If you do this,' Harry said, 'it will change you, and not for the better. Men who have not committed murder are better in every way than men who have. They've not been corrupted by murder, and murder *does* corrupt you. I don't mean the ability to murder – I believe almost any man is capable under the right circumstances – I mean doing the thing itself. You go into it thinking you're one thing, and maybe you are, but you come out of it a different thing altogether. You come out of it changed, colder and harder and more shut off. You have to come out of it that way or else you couldn't live with yourself. It's simply the nature of things.'

'I need to do it. I need to *understand* it.'

'I know,' Harry said. 'I know you *think* that, anyway. I'm just trying to explain to you that it's different than you think.'

'You don't know *what* I think.'

'I don't need to. Whatever it is you think, it's wrong.'

'There's only one way I can find out how it's wrong, though, isn't there?'

Harry nodded. 'I suppose so.'

A thin brunette woman walked over and smiled her red-lipped Joker smile, revealing a large gap between her two front teeth.

'Hi,' she said, 'I'm Delores. I'll be your waitress today. You guys know what you want to drink?'

Harry looked up. 'I'll have a coffee – and I'd love to bum a smoke from you if possible.'

'How'd you know I smoke?'

'Nicotine stains on your fingers,' Harry said.

He pushed his yolk-smeared plate away and picked up the Virginia Slim cigarette he'd bummed off the waitress. He hated that the first cigarette he was smoking in over two decades was a mentholated ladies' cigarette, but he supposed when you weren't buying you couldn't be picky. He stuck it between his lips, grabbed a book of matches from beside the ashtray on the table, made a flame. He brought the match to the end of his cigarette and inhaled, thinking of his first wife's burning corpse – the stench of it, the sight of bubbling flesh turning black and bursting, juices flowing from within as if she were a pig on a spit.

He exhaled through his nostrils.

He'd wondered if it might be harsh after so long, if he might have a coughing fit, but instead it was like going home. It was comfortable and helped to center him.

He sipped his now-cold coffee and looked out the window.

Silas Green had arrived almost thirty minutes earlier – stepped from his vehicle and walked into his office – but Harry hadn't seen him since. The car was still there, and it was still the only car there. Business did not appear to be booming. But then he supposed the private investigation business was probably fairly inconsistent. You'd likely have entire weeks without work, and then suddenly four people would walk in on the same day, each suspecting their spouse of an affair. He also supposed much of the job consisted mainly of telephone calls.

It didn't matter.

'I guess I should talk to you about the algebra of blood,' he said.

'What?'

Harry looked at his son once more. 'The algebra of blood. It was the only way I ever found of justifying myself *to* myself. It has the benefit, I think, of being true.'

He took another sip of his cold coffee, thick and grainy now that he was nearing the bottom of the mug, and followed it with a drag from his cigarette.

'The phrase,' he said, 'comes from some French philosopher, I forget who. He said we must *not* engage in the algebra of blood. But human nature being what it is, we can't help but engage in it. If you look at the big picture, you come to the realization that we do it every day. Every day men and women make blood decisions. They might not think of their decisions in that way, they almost certainly don't, but the consequences of their actions are the same. Day-to-day decisions don't usually draw *much* blood, of course; each person living his life only creates small nicks, shallow wounds, nothing that would draw more response than a paper-cut hiss, but the accumulation of those millions of small wounds among the masses results in the same thing: death. And for what? Mostly the bullshit they fill their lives with. And this isn't judgment. I'm not saying they're *wrong*. I don't think they are. I live the same way. I should have said the bullshit *we* fill our lives with – every single one of us. Because I don't even think there's another way *to* live, not in this world. I'm just saying it is what it is. Enough people buy Japanese cars, a factory in Detroit goes under. The result is hundreds of men out of work – men with wives and children, men with mortgages. Some of them will find work elsewhere, of course, but some of them will become hopeless. Some of them will hang themselves in their closets or blow their brains out. Or maybe intentionally crash their car in order that their death appears to be an accident. They might have life insurance and figure they're worth more to their families dead than alive. They do the math and that's their conclusion. And they're right. Sometimes they're *absolutely* right, despite what some people might say. That's the algebra of blood. It's not profound, and I'm not pretending it is. It's just the way things work. Everyday decisions draw blood. Everyday decisions result in death. People are starving all over the world. Someone with more money than he knows what to do with buys an airplane. That's a blood decision. He could have saved lives, but instead he has his propeller and hundreds of people in some impoverished African country starve to death. And that's okay. It could be he saves lives in some other way and it balances out, but maybe not. It doesn't matter either way because nobody *owes* anybody anything anyway. It's just that pretending you aren't making that decision when you are is lying to yourself, because when you make such a decision you're in effect saying that your own happiness is worth far more than the lives of hundreds of people you don't know and never will. And why wouldn't it be? You're you, after all, the only person you absolutely *have* to give a shit about. A hit is just a more direct route to blood. Hunters who kill for food are the same. Millions of people go to the grocery store every day and buy steaks for dinner and never acknowledge that they're cooking and eating something that was once alive, millions of people who would never walk up to a cow and put a bolt through its brain. But in their way, collectively, they've still done exactly that. Hunters own their kill. They acknowledge it. And when we kill, *we* acknowledge it. We own it. We say to ourselves that this ten thousand dollars I'm getting is worth more than the life of someone I don't know and never will. We say to ourselves that my own safety, the life I'm living, is worth more to me than the life of this person who has threatened my existence, or these *ten* people who have threatened my existence. We do the math explicitly and the blood follows directly. There are no channels that allow us distance. There is no distance that allows us deniability. In its way, it's much more honest than how most people live. It's uglier and it's colder and it's crueler – but it *is* more honest.'

Harry looked down at his cigarette and saw that it had burned all the way to his fingertips. More than an inch of ash hung off the end of it. He tossed it to the ashtray and took a sip of his coffee.

'You do a hit,' he said, 'it's best to simply think of it in those terms. This isn't a person. It's part of a math problem, and you're about to solve it. You put yourself into that mindset and you do your job. You walk away and you feel nothing. If you can do that you'll be able to live with yourself. You'll be less human than you were before – an unavoidable consequence of your actions – but you'll be able to look yourself in the mirror. Just be sure to keep emotion out of it, even emotion that might push you forward. You'd think anger or hatred would be positive emotions in this line of work. They aren't. You don't want to kill for an emotional reason. First, emotion clouds one's thinking and you're more likely to make mistakes. Second, emotions fade. If you can't justify to yourself what you're doing in a cold and clear way, you simply weren't cut out to do this kind of thing. There's no shame in that. You might even take pride in it. It makes you more human than those of us who are capable of inhuman action. But accept it at the outset or you'll be haunted by your actions, for when the hatred and the anger fade what you're left with is guilt and remorse.'

He glanced toward the window and saw the private detective stepping through his front door and walking toward his car.

Though the check had not yet arrived he reached into his wallet, pulled out a twenty – more than sufficient, he was sure – and tossed it to the table.

'It's time to move,' he said.

3

They followed Silas Green to a pawnshop and pulled to the curb across the street as he made a left into the parking lot and brought his car to a stop between two pickup trucks, a red Ford at least a couple decades old and a late-model Dodge Ram. The pawnshop was run-down, the windows filthy and difficult to see through; the vinyl banner hanging from the yellow awning above the store in tatters; the items behind the windows looking as though they might have been collected from dumpsters. Silas Green stepped from his vehicle and walked around to the trunk. From the trunk he removed two violin cases, one much more battered than the other. He slammed the trunk shut and merely stood motionless a moment.

Andrew couldn't see his face, but there was something like sadness or regret in his posture, in the slump of his shoulders. He looked toward the pawnshop's front door, then his feet followed his line of sight, taking him into the place. He dragged his feet while he walked.

The door swung shut behind him slowly as if with a hydraulic sigh.

Andrew's father merely sat behind the wheel, repeatedly tapping out 'Shave and a Haircut' with his fingertips. He didn't speak, but Andrew was glad of that. He was still thinking about what he'd been told at the diner. He was thinking about killing without emotion. He was thinking about doing it as one might change his motor oil or file his taxes.

He reaches for the glove compartment, opens it. Within the glove compartment, on top of the vehicle's owner's manual and some other paperwork, lies a small revolver with a two-inch barrel. He checks the cylinder and finds within it five rounds. The chamber behind the barrel is empty. He'd read a Dashiell Hammett novel as a boy in which a Chinaman kept his gun loaded in that way to prevent an accidental firing. He assumes this one is missing that round for the same reason. He snaps the cylinder back into place and looks toward the pawnshop door. It remains closed. He pushes out of the car. His father asks him, where you going? But he doesn't respond. He simply walks across the street. As he reaches the sidewalk, Silas Green steps from the pawnshop. Instead of two violin cases he is now holding a thin wad of cash – a very thin wad of cash. He flips through it as he steps toward his car, but his expression is sad. His shoulders are slumped. He seems to be thinking more about what he lost in that pawnshop than what he gained. But Andrew pushes that thought away. Only humans can have such feelings as he's attributing to Silas Green and this man is no longer human. He's a problem that must be solved. Andrew approaches him and raises the revolver, thumb on the hammer spur. He doesn't even look up when Andrew thumbs back the hammer and the cylinder rotates, putting a round into the firing position. He's lost in thought. This is good. Andrew doesn't want to make eye contact. This is not a person. It's simply something that must be done. He squeezes the trigger. The revolver kicks toward him while Silas Green's head snaps back in the other direction. A red dot punctuates his forehead just above the left eyebrow, a period which ends the sentence of his life. He fires again, creating a colon. He wonders what will follow that colon on the other side. Thick red liquid oozes from within the man's head. He lets go of the wad of cash. A breeze scatters the bills, then carries them away. Andrew watches as they flutter across the asphalt like autumn leaves. Then a heavy sound brings him back to Silas Green. The man has collapsed and now lies dead on the ground, blood pooling beneath his head.

Andrew turns back toward his father's car. He walks across the street. He raises the gun and aims it at his father's face.

His father looks back at him with his pale sad eyes. 'Do you really think you can do it?'

Rage builds within him and hatred. He thumbs back the hammer. Tears stream down his face. His hand begins to shake uncontrollably. His face balls up with emotion. His whole body feels tense. He can barely see through the tears of his kaleidoscope eyes. He tries to make himself squeeze the trigger, but something within him will not allow it. He doesn't know why. He needs to do this. He needs to do this. Do it, you fucking piece of shit. Do it. He's not your father, he's an obstacle. He's simply the skin you must shed in order that you might become yourself, and there's only one way to do that. This is that way.

So do it already.

He drops his arm.

'Goddamn it,' he whispers to himself under his breath. 'Fuck.'

His father smiles but his eyes remain sad. 'You don't have it, son. You don't have it, and you should be glad you don't.'

The pawnshop's front door swung open. Silas Green stepped out into the sun. In his right hand he held a fold of cash, which he slipped into his pocket. Then he continued toward his car, pulled open the door, and fell in behind the wheel. He lit a cigarillo. He started his car. He pulled out into the street.

Andrew's father put his car into gear and pulled out into the street behind him. He followed from a distance. He didn't speak. His face was calm.

4

Harry watched the car in front of him and thought about the man within it. He was a punk – there was no denying that – but he was also shifty. If he believed Harry really was coming after him – and there was no reason he shouldn't; Harry had told him he was – he was likely to do something desperate to save his own skin.

So far as Harry could tell, there were only three moves the man could make – possibly four – and only one with any real chance of getting him out of his situation free and clear. The question was whether Silas Green could see far enough into the future to know what that move was. Harry would have to assume the answer was yes until he found out otherwise. If he underestimated the man he might end up dead, and he might end up getting Andrew killed as well. Or worse, he might get Andrew killed and live to know about it.

Maybe he should have simply walked into the man's office this morning and done him there. It would have eliminated the possibility of complications. Of course it also would have increased the likelihood of his getting caught. Killing a man in this day and age was very different from when he'd last taken the breath from someone's lungs. Crime scene investigations were more advanced. Things that twenty-six years ago would not have been evidence could now put a man in prison for the rest of his life.

No, he needed to do this right despite the risk of complications.

There was no way around it.

And if things did get complicated he'd simply have to deal with them as best he could. For fifteen years he had committed acts which could have ended his life as a free man – for fifteen years he'd been the primary suspect even for crimes he hadn't committed, his reputation being what it was – and yet he still walked the streets. It was true that decades had passed since he last did anything remotely illegal. It was true that he was rusty and old. But he believed it was also true that if it came down to it instinct would take over and carry him through.

He hoped so, anyway.

Silas Green pulled into the parking lot of a convenience store. Harry swerved to the curb across the street. He watched the man disappear into the store, and he waited. He waited for what felt a very long time. He felt anxious and impatient.

After over twenty minutes he began to wonder if the man had spotted him and stolen out the back door. He might have ditched his car and decided to go where he was going on foot. He might not have, of course, but if he *had* Harry wanted to know about it. He wanted to know what was going on, and something was going on. Nobody spent that amount of time shopping in such a place. Convenience stores were where you went for cigarettes or to buy a six pack, not to fill your refrigerator for the week. They were two-minute stops not twenty.

He pushed open the driver side door and stepped from the vehicle.

'Wait here,' he said, swinging the door shut.

He waited by the car for traffic to clear, and once there was a break in the flow of cars and trucks and SUVs, walked toward the convenience store. He looked in through a window before entering and saw that – with the exception of a young fellow behind the counter – the place appeared to be empty.

He pushed through the glass door, strolled around the place, and found that it was in fact empty. The private detective was not sitting on his haunches reading the ingredients of a low-set box of cookies or leaning down to grab a quart of motor oil. He simply wasn't here.

But Harry'd suspected he wouldn't be here, so he was hardly surprised.

He glanced at the doors leading into the back, then walked toward them.

As he was pushing his way through the man behind the counter told him you can't go back there, man, but there was a question in his tone, as if he wasn't sure of what he was saying.

'I'm just looking for the bathroom,' Harry said, and continued.

The doors swung shut behind him.

He found himself standing in a large stockroom. Stacks of Coke and beer and candy bars and canned foods lined the walls, teetering toward the water-stained acoustic ceiling. Empty boxes were piled in various places. Mouse turds punctuated the concrete floor despite the mouse traps laid about, dead mice in at least two of them. Cobwebs clung to the corners.

But no Silas Green.

Harry walked toward a gray metal door leading out back, grabbed the handle, turned it. He pushed his way out into the sunlight, looking left, then right down a patchy asphalt alleyway. There was no sign of Silas Green. If he'd made his way out through this door – and Harry suspected he had – he was in the wind now.

He pushed his way back into the fluorescent-lighted store.

'Couldn't find a bathroom.'

'We don't have a public bathroom.'

Harry shrugged, walked toward the refrigerators, pulled a Coke from one of them. It felt cool in his sweaty palm. He walked with it to the counter and set it down.

'That be all?'

'Pack of Camel Filters,' he said, grabbing a small plastic lighter. 'And this.'

He sat down in the car, peeled the cellophane from his cigarettes, pulled out the foil. He brought the pack to his face, pinched a filter between his teeth, pulled the pack away save one cigarette which dangled from his lip. He lit that cigarette and inhaled deeply. It tasted good. It tasted like his past – no, not like *his* past. Harry White had never smoked a day in his life. Harry Combs, on the other hand, had gone through two packs a day for over a decade.

He wondered whether to wait here or head back to Silas Green's office. The man had left his car, which meant he had to return at some point, but if he'd spotted Harry and wanted to ditch him, that meant he was doing something he didn't want Harry to know about, and that was just the sort of thing Harry *needed* to know about.

Or maybe the man was still inside. He very well could be. Harry hadn't considered that he might be hiding behind boxes or crates in the stockroom, simply hoping Harry left.

Then there was the possibility that he hadn't even seen Harry, but was simply meeting with someone. He had just pawned a couple violins. He had just pawned stuff that fit within violin cases, anyway. He could be paying the vigorish on a loan, trying to buy himself more time. He could also be attempting to talk his way out of debt completely. If that was the case he was talking Harry *into* trouble even as he was talking himself out of it – trying to, anyway – and if his jaw was moving in such an attempt Harry knew just what the man was saying. Trouble didn't vanish, after all; it was merely transferred or delayed.

Harry would simply have to wait and hope that Silas Green's expression when he next saw the man might tell him something.

'I got you a Coke,' he said, handing the bottle to Andrew.

'Thanks.' Andrew untwisted the cap and took a swallow.

Harry wished he'd not said anything to the private detective, wished he'd not made any threats. That would have eliminated this worry. But he lost his temper, and now the situation was what it was. That is why you don't allow emotion into this sort of thing. That is why you must be a professional. He'd failed to follow his own advice.

But whatever happened he'd deal with it.

He'd try to.

5

Andrew was halfway through his Coke when Silas Green emerged from the convenience store. His hands were stuffed into his pockets and he was strolling, casual, a toothy grin on his bandaged face. Andrew wondered what had happened to make him smile. Up to now he'd looked simultaneously tired and frightened. There'd been a weariness in his posture. But something had happened. Something had changed.

His father took a final drag of his third cigarette and flicked it out the window.

Under his breath he cursed.

'What is it?'

'That goddamn smile.'

'What does it mean?'

'Trouble.'

'How?'

His father didn't answer. He merely started the car and put it into gear.

'What kind of trouble are we talking about?'

'The serious kind.'

He pulled the car out into the street and followed behind the private detective.

6

Harry followed the private detective back to his office on Preston Highway and once more parked across the street. He still didn't know how he was going to take care of the man – how he was going to instruct Andrew to take care of him – but he knew his threat had likely caused trouble. He couldn't believe he'd lost control of himself in that way.

If he'd simply kept his cool he could have handled this easily. He could have killed the man without him ever knowing what was coming.

It also occurred to him now that he'd have to break into the office across the street at some point. He'd wanted to avoid going anywhere near it. He'd wanted to avoid even the possibility of leaving traces of himself behind at the scene, but if he didn't break into the place he'd almost certainly be leaving all sorts of evidence of his existence behind – much more than he could possibly leave behind in any attempt to eliminate that evidence. Even if the police couldn't tie him to this murder they'd be able to tie him to what happened in Dallas, for Harry was certain there was evidence within that office that proved he was Harry Combs.

Or he could simply burn the place down. Fire, after all, was the ultimate cleanser.

Either way, he'd have to take care of it.

He'd forgotten how these things could fall like houses of cards. He'd forgotten that one false move, one lapse in judgment, one oversight could bring the whole thing down on you. This was why you had to keep your cool. A shaky hand could ruin you.

Still, today was not the day to handle that.

The man left his office at half past six. Harry started his car, pulled into the street, and followed him north on Preston Highway for a few miles before he turned right onto Hess. This was a narrow two-lane street without much traffic, so Harry dropped back to avoid being spotted. They drove nearly all the way to Poplar Level Road – passing several houses and an elementary school – before cutting right onto a narrow residential street.

The private detective pulled his car into a driveway and killed the engine. He stepped from his vehicle. He walked across his grass to the front porch of a small woodsided house, up three steps, and then vanished through a white-painted front door.

This was where he lived.

If he was neither married nor in possession of children

it might be feasible to do the job here, but it was still Harry's second choice. If the private detective went missing – and murdered people tended to do that – there would be a police investigation. An investigation might turn up evidence of the murder, bloodstains which could not be washed out completely, bullet holes in the walls or floor or ceiling.

No, it would be best to do the job in a location that had no connection to the man. It would be best to do it neither in his office nor in his home. If the location had no connection to the private detective the police would never think to bring a crime scene unit there.

Yet if it came to that Harry now knew where he lived. That was enough for now.

He started the car.

THEN:

In early October, while renting a small house in Butchertown about fifty yards from the Ohio, he sits down to write his first letter. He knows it's a mistake – knows he is risking his life – but he doesn't care. For months now he has lived as Harry White, and Harry White is a man with nothing and nobody – he is a man completely isolated: some men, he's found, are islands *– and he doesn't know how he might become something else, doesn't know how he might collect the things which normal men possess, which normal men have simply because they have lived their lives. Family, friends, coworkers. People who care for you and about whom you can care.*

A history you can own.

Before becoming this new person he'd had no idea just how lonely this life might be. He should have, but knowing you are losing everything and living with nothing happen to be two very different things, the former being only an idea while the latter is hard reality.

There are people in town who now recognize him – a wait-ress at his favorite restaurant; a teller at Fifth-Third Bank who smiles and says nice to see you again, Mr White, when he pushes in through the door; his barber – but mostly he is alone. He has no one to call if he should want company while throw-ing back a few at one of the local bars. He has no one to be angry at him for failing to refill the ice cube tray or forgetting to take out the trash. The walls of his rented house hold no pictures.

So he sits down to write a letter in order to feel, if only briefly, connected to those who existed in his old life back when he was a different person. As he types he wonders how much Andrew has grown. Probably he fits none of the clothes he was wearing when Harry had to leave. Probably he has begun to use the potty. Probably he is now using entire phrases rather than single words and gestures.

He wonders if there was a service for Helen. He wonders what Helen's brother Dave, whom he has always liked, might think of him now. If she had died under different circumstances the two of them could have had a few drinks together and talked about her. Instead Dave probably wishes that he were dead – would probably try to kill him if they were to meet again.

Feeling as he does, he might let him.

When the letter is finished he folds it around five hundred dol-lars and slips it into an envelope, which he then seals, stamps, and labels.

If he knew what mailing this letter would lead to, if he knew that almost twenty-six years from now his son would find the letter and come out to see him, and in seeing him decide he must die, decide to make him die, he might never drive across the river and drop it into a mailbox. Then again, feeling as he does, he might.

But what he might do is irrelevant, because, being human, he has no special knowledge of future events. It is nothing but a gray smudge on the horizon. So he mails the letter, and what happens as a result of that happens.

Small actions sometimes have big consequences while big actions sometimes have none.

You never know.

NOW:

1

Andrew sat in the car while his father drove. He felt sick to his stomach. He felt sick about doing what he'd told his father he wanted to do. He didn't know if he had it in him. He feared that he didn't. Part of him wished there were a way out of this situation, a way out that required nothing of him.

His father puts a cigarette between his lips while he drives, taking his eyes off the road. He thumbs a lighter but no flame emerges.

The light ahead turns yellow.

He thumbs the wheel again and again without achieving fire. He curses under his breath. Finally, an orange glow emerges. He brings it to the end of his cigarette. He inhales.

The light turns red but his father sees it too late. He speeds into the intersection just before a Mack truck hauling a Kroger trailer does the same. The truck comes from the left. Its horn blares. Both Andrew and his father look in that direction. The driver's face is a mask of shock.

Then the truck is upon them.

The noise is thunderous, the impact great. It flips the car over two and a half times, and once it has stopped rolling it goes sliding on its roof toward – toward somewhere. It is all a blur of noise and fury and pain. The world has simply gone mad. A moment ago everything was normal, but now the world is pure insanity. The car crashes into something, a building or a telephone pole or another car, and stops hard.

Andrew can hear liquid dripping and glass shards falling to the ground. His arm throbs with pain and when he looks down at it he sees it's bent at a strange, unnatural angle. His forearm seems to have developed an extra elbow.

Then he looks toward his father.

The man's neck is broken and his head has been smashed in. Blood puddles beneath it on the roof of the car, soaking into the beige headliner.

Despite the pain Andrew feels happiness well up within him.

His father is dead. The man is dead and he had to do nothing to make it happen.

The burden is gone – gone.

'What are you thinking about?'

Andrew glanced toward his father.

'What?'

'What are you thinking about?'

'Nothing.'

His father nodded, looked away.

2

Harry looked back toward the road and thought about what might come next. It could be nothing – that was a distinct possibility – but he knew he had to prepare for more than that. He could not go through the evening as if nothing would happen, not while suspecting that the private detective had transferred his problems. If he ignored his suspicions and something *did* happen he was in trouble, possibly in serious trouble. For he didn't know who he might be dealing with, didn't know how serious he or they might be.

Bottom line was, he'd have to make preparations.

He turned onto his street and drove to his house, rolling past several similar houses – nice brick Cape Cods in which nothing untoward could possibly happen. He parked the car on the street and stepped from the vehicle, stepped out into the evening.

Preparedness, after all, was what the unprepared called luck.

Teresa wasn't at the kitchen table when he walked into the room. His first thought was that they had come, whoever they were. They had already come and made their move. They'd kidnapped Teresa and were holding her for the money they knew he had. But he pushed the thought away, pushed it into the shadowed corners of his mind where it might be covered in darkness, and walked out of the room. He looked in the downstairs bathroom but the room was empty. Then he looked in the bedroom, and there he found her.

She was sitting up in bed. Though it was almost eighty degrees inside, the blankets were pulled up to her neck. Her face was glossy with sweat. When he walked into the room she looked toward him with her large green eyes. They were wide and rheumy, though not he thought with drink. She seemed, in fact, to be suffering from the opposite.

'Are you out of vodka?'

'No.'

'What's wrong?'

'I'm – I'm trying to quit.' She smiled at him, or tried to, but it came across as a pained and sickly grimace. Her skin was pale, her body shaking at every muscle and joint.

'You should have one drink,' he said, 'just to calm this reaction. Quitting all at once is dangerous when you drink as much as you do.'

She shook her head. 'I won't.'

'Why?'

'Because if I start I won't stop. You know that.'

He couldn't understand what had happened, why she

had chosen today to quit drinking. But he knew she was serious about it. One does not sit through what she was sitting through and refuse a drink if one is not serious. But *why* was she serious? What was she thinking?

He didn't know.

'Listen,' he said, 'I need you and Andrew to stay in a motel tonight.'

'Why?'

'Something's happened – something *might* have happened – and I don't want either of you to be in any danger.'

'Not tonight, Harry.'

'I was thinking the same thing.'

'What?'

'I can't change things now, Teresa.'

'I just want to stay in bed and get through this.'

'Have a drink to calm your nerves. I'll pack an overnight bag.'

'Don't undermine this,' she said. She said it with force, tears standing out in her tired bloodshot eyes.

'I'm not trying to undermine anything,' he said.

'You *are*.'

'I'm trying to keep you safe.'

'Pack me a bag,' she said. 'But I'm *not* drinking.'

'Okay,' he said. Then he said it again.

3

Andrew stood in the driveway with his arms crossed and watched as his father helped his shaking wife to the car and got her into it – gently, as if she were a china doll. He kissed her sweaty forehead and said I love you, then he shut the door and lit a cigarette.

'Why are you sending me away?'

The man took a drag from his cigarette and looked toward him.

'If something happens here tonight,' he said, 'it will be easier for me to take care of it alone. I don't want to have to worry about you and Teresa.'

'You don't have to worry about me.'

'If I thought it would be beneficial to have you here I'd have you stay. It wouldn't be. If the only person here I give a damn about is me – and then just barely – I can remain focused. I need that. I need to do what must be done without second-guessing my decisions.'

'I can take care of myself.'

'That isn't the issue.'

'Then why are you sending me away with a useless old woman?'

'I already told you why, Andrew.'

'It sounded like bullshit to me.'

'It wasn't.'

Andrew closed his eyes in order to find focus, in order

to push the anger down and allow thought to enter his mind. He felt he was being treated as a little boy. He was being sent away with an alcoholic old woman rather than being trusted to handle himself as a man. And he *was* a man, goddamn it.

It wasn't right. It wasn't *at all* right.

Yet there was a part of him that didn't know whether he could handle what might be coming. He thought that when it came down to it he'd be able to take care of Silas Green, but that would happen under controlled circumstances, and probably from a distance. He had no idea what would happen here tonight. But that doubtful part of him only served to make him more angry. It made him hate himself for being less than he should be, for being weak. This was one area in which his father was the better man. He was old and broken down, but displayed only sureness, confidence. He knew what to do and how to do it, whereas Andrew felt lost.

He was full of anger and hatred, but he was also full of fear and confusion.

He just wanted to be done with this. He wanted it to be over so that he could finally feel some sense of closure. He wanted only to look at it over his shoulder. Instead it remained right in front of him; it seemed always to remain in front of him no matter how far he went, like the horizon, and he didn't know *when* he might finally be able to pass it.

But this fight would not get him there. It was not important. He was reacting irrationally, and his reaction might cause his father to stop trusting him. The man could begin thinking he had too much anger inside to handle dealing with Silas Green, and that couldn't happen. He needed to do that. He needed to know that he was *capable* of it. Before he tried anything with his father he needed to know he could squeeze a trigger when necessary, otherwise he'd never have the courage to do what he needed to do.

And he needed his father there to help him through it. This first time he *needed* that.

He opened his eyes.

'You're right,' he said. 'I lost my temper and I shouldn't have.'

'I'll see you tomorrow,' his father said.

'I hope so.' But part of him hoped he wouldn't. Part of him hoped that whatever happened tonight would end his father. He might not feel the same as he would if he'd done it himself, but it would still provide some sense of closure, some sense of an ending, and from the ashes he could grow a new beginning.

After all, every man grows in the soil under which his father is buried.

4

Harry sat in darkness. Across his lap lay a chopped base-ball bat, better for close quarters than a full-sized one. He had his pistol upstairs, but if something happened and the police found a round, or if he had to discard the gun for some reason and they found it, they might be able to trace it back to Dallas. If that happened, they'd know Harry Combs was in Louisville. They might not know where he was exactly, but it wouldn't take long for them to find him. No, this was safer than using the gun he had – or trying to procure one in a town where he was known and respected. The last thing he needed was tongues wagging.

His stomach felt sour, his chest tight. He knew very well that he might sit in this chair all night waiting for nothing, but he didn't care. He'd rather do this and face only silence than be unprepared and face something more dangerous, something real.

He wished he knew what was going through Teresa's head, what she was thinking. He wished he knew what had caused her to decide to quit the booze, to attempt it at any rate. He wondered why part of him hoped she failed.

For years he had worried about her, about both her mind and her health. He'd been afraid that he might come home and find her dead on the kitchen floor. But he'd also kept her vodka supply well stocked, and he'd never said a word no matter how bad it got, and there were months, even years, when it was very bad indeed.

And tonight he tried to talk her into drinking. What he'd said made sense – it *was* dangerous to quit suddenly when you'd been drinking as heavily as she had for as long as she had – but that it made sense was irrelevant. He knew himself well enough to know that wasn't why he'd wanted her to have a drink.

Unfortunately, he didn't know the real reason. It was buried behind muddled emotion and confused motives. It was buried deep.

He was afraid it had something to do with control.

Sometimes he wished he knew himself better. But knowledge of self could be dangerous. The lights were out in the darkest corners of your mind for a reason.

There were things there that no one was meant to see.

Several cars passed on the street, but none of them stopped. The house creaked, but because of no presence. The clocks of the world ticked. He fell asleep several times, but only briefly, his head dropping to his chest before quickly snapping up again, eyes wide. The tense feeling within him dissipated, working its way to his extremities and leaving his body through his fingertips and toes.

He was waiting for nothing; that's what he came to believe.

Then a car moved on the street but did not pass.

Instead it came to a stop and the engine went silent. Car doors opened and closed.

His fist gripped the baseball bat.

He'd not swung one of these in thirty years, but he had a feeling he was going to do so tonight, if only to make it clear that he'd not be fucked with. He wondered how much had stayed with him. How much he was capable of, so much older and slower and broken-down now than once he'd been.

Feet thudded up the concrete steps outside.

Who's that walking on my bridge?

There were two sets of them, four feet moving along, and they were the footsteps of large men walking with purpose.

This was it then.

The question now was how it would go down, and a lot of that depended on how he behaved, how they perceived him. Men like this were animals. They didn't think. They felt and reacted. What they felt about him mattered and mattered greatly, for it would affect their reaction. If they thought he could be pushed they would push. If they thought he was a wall, however, they might simply turn away.

He closed his eyes and tried to find his center.

The footsteps stopped at his front door. A knock followed.

He opened his eyes.

*

He looked through the peephole at two men in Brooks Brothers suits. They were bulky and the suits were ill-fitting, tight around their arms and thighs and barrel chests. The one on the left looked to have a pistol tucked into his pants.

He inhaled and exhaled.

His index finger tapped nervously on the bat gripped in his right hand.

With his left he reached out and grabbed the deadbolt, turned it. It stopped turning with a click, bolt retracted.

He turned the knob and pulled open the front door to find himself looking at the two men through the glass of his storm door. They looked back from dull eyes like unpolished stones planted in their square heads.

'How much does he owe?'

Neither man spoke.

Harry repeated himself: 'How much does he owe?'

Finally the one on the right answered: 'Thirteen thousand.'

Harry nodded. 'Now tell me how that has anything to do with me.'

'He said you had it.'

'And more.'

'Lots of people have it, but you aren't knocking on their doors.'

'When you go duck hunting, you don't aim at the flock. You pick your bird.'

'You picked the wrong bird. I'm not going down.'

'Big talk.'

'Go back to your car and you might live through the night.'

The one on the right laughed humorlessly. The one on the left reached for his piece with one hand and the storm door with the other. He pulled open the door and started in.

He'd only managed to get one foot onto the hardwood floor before Harry swung the bat, cracking the man in the side of the head.

He swung with such force that it stung his palm badly and bounced back toward him a good distance.

The impact made a wet cracking sound.

The man fell to his knees.

Harry swung again, ignoring his pain, and landed a blow on the back of the man's skull, which sounded like something breaking through the icy surface of a frozen pond – a hard crack followed quickly by a wet sound beneath.

The man fell forward, unconscious. The gun dropped from his hand, a weapon Harry didn't recognize, with a silencer screwed into it.

Harry grabbed it quickly and swung around to the second man.

He was already aiming his own silenced pistol at Harry, a pistol Harry hadn't known he'd had. But of course he'd come armed. Men like this always did.

A wry grin lit up his hard face. 'You got moxie, old man.'

'I've got a lot of things.'

'At least a hundred thousand of them according to Silas Green. If I knew where you had them hidden you'd be dead already.'

'You said he owed thirteen.'

'We wouldn't be here for thirteen.'

'You're not here for anything.'

'I beg to differ.'

'A man shouldn't beg.'

'Put down the gun.'

'You're walking away empty-handed or you aren't walking away at all.'

'I'll tell you one more time: put down the gun.'

Harry looked down to the man sprawled across his floor. Blood trickled down his thick neck. He pointed the pistol at the back of his head and pulled the trigger. The gun kicked in his hand and smoke wafted from the silencer. The man's head jerked away. A flap of hair and bone hinged out the other side like a door.

'Jesus *fuck*.'

'Like I said: you walk away empty-handed or you don't walk away at all. Collect your corpse and get the fuck out of here.'

The man stared at him wide-eyed for a long moment.

'Who the fuck *are* you?'

'Harry White. I run a bookshop on Bardstown Road. If

you know what's good for you, you'll let me live my life in peace.'

'You'll find peace all right.'

The man raised his gun to take aim at Harry's face.

Harry knocked the arm aside and smashed him in the nose with the butt of his pistol. The man started to stumble backwards, but Harry grabbed his collar and yanked him into the house. He turned toward Harry, prepared to attack, and Harry hit him again. He didn't want to shoot the man in the head while he stood. The blood spatter would be a bitch to clean up, spread across green curtains, white walls, and the pictures which hung there.

He aimed at the man's right foot instead and pulled the trigger.

The man yelled out and fell to the floor.

Harry pulled the trigger again, this time aiming for a kill, and when he did he felt nothing – nothing at all.

5

Andrew sat on his bed and stared at the television but had no idea what was happening onscreen. To his mind it was nothing but flashing lights, color and noise. He was thinking about his father. He was thinking about the strange mix of emotions stirred up every time he saw the man. Part of him still wondered whether he was even his son – but deep inside he knew he was. He *had* to be. He wondered again – as he often did – whether he'd be able to go through with it when the time came.

He told himself he would. He told himself he didn't have a choice.

It was the only way he'd ever shed his father's skin – unless in attempting to do so he *became* his father.

No: he was nothing like his father.

That's right, Andrew. You're weaker than him. You're smaller than him.

But he might become like his father if he committed this act, for wasn't it a crime equal to any of his father's? How would he be any different if he did this?

But it was the only way he could think to finally finish all this. The only way to finally expel all of this noxious emotion pent up within him. It was contaminating him. This was the only way to release himself fully so that he might fully become himself.

'You're not as smart as you think.'

He looked toward Teresa. She was sitting on a bed about three feet from his. The blankets were pulled up to her neck. She was shaking. Her skin looked jaundiced. She looked, in fact, about half a step from death. One small nudge and she'd fall into it.

'Excuse me?'

'You might have your father fooled but I see through you.'

The intensity of her stare made him drop his eyes.

'I don't know what you're talking about.'

'You know exactly what I'm talking about.'

Andrew laughed and shook his head.

'I see through you. I know how you look at him when you think he's not looking back. I can see what's behind your eyes. I might be a useless old woman, but I know what you are, and sooner or later Harry will figure it out too. You won't be able to fool him forever. He's smarter than you – and he's better than you.'

Andrew laughed again his false laugh and said: 'You're crazy.'

But he didn't believe she was. She was more aware of the situation and more perceptive than he ever would have suspected – she sat drunkenly in the kitchen seeming to process nothing when in reality she processed and understood everything – and her words hit him hard.

He'd not even considered that his father might not *allow* himself to be killed. He hadn't thought of the fact that if his father managed to see through him before the time came to act he might turn on him, and with an arctic coldness.

But that was a big if. His father was blind – his father wanted his son back so badly he was blind to everything else – and that eventually would kill him, for when you can't see what's coming it's bound to hit you square.

The telephone rang.

*

When he opened the front door he found his father hunched over a corpse, taping a trash bag over the bloody mess that was once its head. A second corpse lay on the floor, a white trash bag already covering the gore created above its neck. Blood was visible through the plastic, smeared across the insides like raspberry jam. The wood floor was also smeared and spattered with blood, thick and somehow gelatinous.

'What happened?' he said, feeling sick to his stomach.

'I think that's obvious.' His father looked up at him, duct tape in hand, eyes cold and dark as a winter night. 'Can you go to the garage and get me a couple tarps? They should be on the shelf in the back right corner next to the Christmas decorations.'

6

Harry drove a black Cadillac toward the river. He glanced in his rearview mirror and saw a pair of headlights in the darkness. The bodies lay silent in his trunk. After twenty-six years he had killed again, and it was strange in that it didn't feel at all strange. He felt calm. He merely had to take care of business, which was what he was doing. It was simple as that.

When he got where he was going he parked. The car which had been tailing him parked to the left. The small lot was otherwise empty.

He stepped from his vehicle and lit a cigarette. He looked up at the moon. It seemed so peaceful up there, so free of pain and worry, so free of trouble.

If he could live on the moon, if he could take Teresa and fly up there away from all this, he thought he might do it. He knew it was a childish thought – the thought of a small boy, really – but it was a true thought too.

Things would be simple up there.

Even his relationship with Andrew was causing him worry. He wanted so desperately for them to have something bordering on a normal relationship, but he no longer believed that was possible. What they were doing here tonight was evidence of that. They would never play catch in the backyard. They'd never grill meat on a summer day, not while feeling carefree and happy. They were here not to spend the day fishing but to dispose of bodies.

They shared not the normal things that father and son shared but death.

Blood was the glue which held them together, blood which flowed from the wounds of those slain and left behind, not love. They overlapped only in violence. Otherwise, as this week had shown him, they had very little to talk about.

Otherwise they were strangers. They shared the same face, much of the same makeup, but they were strangers nonetheless.

They didn't have to be – not at the beginning – but the distance between them now was too great ever to close.

Harry walked to the trunk and keyed it open. Within he found two large bundles wrapped in tarps and bound with rope. They lay there motionless, stuffed and contorted like so much luggage – and why not? They were no longer people. They were only meat.

He was surprised he managed to stuff them both in there.

Of course, he'd had to remove the spare.

7

Andrew helped his father drag the bodies down a hill through a line of trees to the rocky shore of the Ohio River. It was a peaceful night, and this late it was a cool one, but he wished to be anywhere but here, wished to be doing anything but this. He'd wanted to be a part of this but now that he was he didn't like it at all.

He wanted to be home with Melissa. He wanted to be asleep in her arms.

He hated his father, but as they spent time together he found that he also loved him in a strange way. The man had given him life, and there'd been a time when he could easily have taken it back but had not. He also found that he respected him. That he had not at all expected.

Melissa was right.

You do not find clarity by stirring up the mud of your past.

Instead you find confusion. You find pain. You find that your hatred is tinged with both love and respect.

Yet he still intended to follow through with this. He intended to see his father dead, love or no, for what was love when combined with hatred but an obligation you didn't want to keep?

He needed to close the door he had opened, and there is no lock on a door like death. It's the only kind that can't be picked. Once you're dead the door is closed forever.

'Grab some rocks,' his father said, untying one of the tarps.

'What for?'

'We need to weigh these things down.'

Andrew leaned over and picked up a large stone.

He walks toward his father with it gripped in his fist. His father looks up at him and asks, what are you doing? Ending this, he says, and swings toward his father's head. The stone hits his temple with a moist crack. His father falls to his side, unconscious. He falls atop a corpse which lies there like an unwrapped present. Andrew falls upon him, hitting him with the stone again and again. Hitting him until he's unrecognizable. Hitting him until his head is like a leather sack holding glass shards and rotten meat, his skull broken and broken again.

His brutally extracted teeth lie on the blue tarp like malformed pearls.

He picked up a second stone, then a third and a fourth and a fifth, loading them into the crook of his arm. He carried them to the corpse and threw them atop it. Then he stopped moving and looked down at the body which lay before him.

Once this had been a man. Once this had been someone with hopes and dreams. Some loving mother had squeezed it from her womb and nursed it at her breast. Now it was man-shaped meat and nothing more. Take away thought of what it once had been and what were you left with? The human equivalent of a side of beef. And cows were slaughtered every day.

How many steaks had he eaten in his lifetime?

He looked toward his father and believed he could do it.

He would make certain first. He would take care of the private detective in order to be sure of himself. In order to do it first with the support of someone experienced in the trade. But he thought he'd be able to do it himself when the time came.

Why not?

Like cows, people died every day. What did it matter how it happened?

The answer was simple: it didn't.

Most of the time it didn't.

How his mother was killed, though, that still mattered a great deal.

8

They dumped the bodies into the river, Harry hoping that a fisherman didn't catch his line on one of the tarps. Not that it would matter much. Nobody fished the Ohio with test weight strong enough to land a man of two hundred pounds, and what was a broken line to him?

Anyway, with luck the current would carry the bodies down the river a good distance before they finally settled and found their resting places. If they were eventually discovered no one would know *where* they'd been dropped into the water, and they'd be so badly decayed it would be difficult to determine their identities – fingerprints would be rotted away, and Harry had already disposed of their wallets and knocked their teeth from their mouths.

'Okay,' he said. 'Let's deal with the car.'

Harry drove the Cadillac to the west end of Louisville and Andrew followed. He skirted around darkened side streets looking for an isolated location, someplace time didn't move quite as quickly, finally settling on an out-of-business gas station. The sign had been removed, as had the pumps. The windows of the store proper were covered in graffiti. Trash was littered across the asphalt – old cups, discarded items of clothing, newspapers, a tire.

Harry drove the car around to the far side of the

station where it wouldn't be seen from the street. Then he parked and stepped out into the night.

After a moment he opened the back door of the car and removed a gas can from the floorboard. Up until a couple hours ago this was gasoline intended for his lawn-mower. Now it would serve an entirely different purpose. He popped the cap off and began dousing the cloth interior, then the roof and the hood and the trunk. When the gas can was nearly empty he poured a trail on the asphalt, backing away about twenty feet. He thumbed his lighter, sat on his haunches, and brought the orange flame to the trail of gasoline. It ignited immediately, and the flame rushed toward the car, then the car itself ignited.

Black smoke began to billow above it, forming a pillar to hold up the night.

Harry carried the gas can toward Andrew's car, pulled open the passenger side door, and got inside.

'Let's head home,' he said.

His son nodded and put the car into gear.

9

'Head on back to the motel,' his father said, 'get yourself a couple hours' sleep, and I'll see you and Teresa back here at nine.'

Andrew nodded. He wasn't sure he had words left in

him after the night he'd had. He felt raw and sick, yet when he looked at his father – who had done most of the ugly things which were done tonight – the man looked calm and focused.

It was inhuman.

He turned and walked toward his car. When he reached it he pulled open the door.

'Andrew.'

He looked toward his father.

'Good work tonight.'

He nodded again and fell into his vehicle.

10

Harry walked into the house and looked at the bloody mess spread across his living-room floor. He wished he could simply go to bed – he was tired – but he still had to take care of this. He walked to the kitchen and grabbed spray cleaner, a roll of paper towels, and a trash bag.

Once the blood was wiped up he grabbed a kitchen knife. One of the bullets had imbedded itself in the floor and he needed to get it out.

Soon enough he had.

He plugged the hole with wood filler. It didn't quite match but it was close enough. No one but him would notice it, for no one but him would look for it.

He poured bleach into the trash bag and shook it

around, then he carried it back to his trash can and threw it inside.

If someone found it before pick-up day it would be suspicious, of course, but so far he was still beyond suspicion as far as the Louisville Police Department was concerned, and he could think of nothing – yet – that might draw him to their attention. He'd had no connection to these men. They were career criminals. He was a quiet bookseller. There were sure to be a dozen people or more the police would go to before even thinking of him, and probably they'd never think of him, even if they did find the bodies and manage to identify them.

He walked back inside and looked around the living room. It was clean and tidy and perfectly middle class. It was just the way it should be.

So he walked to his bedroom, kicked off his shoes, and crawled into bed. Light was already seeping in through the blinds. The digital clock on the nightstand told him it was half past six in the morning.

He cursed and put a pillow over his face to block the light.

He had to get up an hour and a half from now. He thought about simply remaining awake. A small amount of sleep could be worse than no sleep at all, making you groggy and disoriented and unfocused in a way you would not be had you remained awake. He could find something on television and watch it for a while. He formed an image of his television in his mind. On the screen he pictured himself lying down. He was wearing nothing. A sheet covered his body and the sheet was cool. The room was dark. He didn't move.

He fell into sleep.

THEN:

He meets Teresa in the spring of 1967. They are both still fairly young – Harry now forty, she in her late thirties – but they both have serious histories, tragic histories, as Harry will soon learn. It's part of what ties them together.

He's sitting in a bar hunched over his whiskey when she walks up beside him and orders a tall screwdriver. Her voice is cute – slightly nasal, almost little-girlish – and it causes him to glance over in her direction. Short dark hair frames a heart-shaped face. Her lips are full and nicely shaped. Her brown almond eyes sparkle with life. She is, in fact, even cuter than her voice.

She must feel him looking at her, for she glances back. For a moment her expression is flat, then she decides to smile. It makes her even more beautiful, though she seems completely unaware of just how attractive she is, for she doesn't carry herself in that arrogant way beautiful women often do.

'Can I buy your drink?'

'Buy your own,' she says.

'Can I buy you your drink?'

'Oh, in that case . . .'

She takes the stool beside his.

'Harry White,' he says.

'Teresa Pemberton.'

'Nice to meet you.'

'We'll see about that.'

Her drink arrives and she sucks it through a straw. By the time she pulls her lips away the glass contains only orange-coated ice.

Ten minutes later they're sitting at a table in the corner and Teresa is laughing at an idiotic joke he told about a conversation between two sausages in a frying pan. He laughs with her, not at his own joke but her reaction to it, which is genuine and complete. He can tell that at the moment nothing else exists for her but her laughter, and it's wonderful and infectious laughter indeed.

Even he can get lost in it.

Not since Helen died – and, honestly, for years before that – has he experienced a single emotion purely. With Helen everything was tinged with regrets and anger, even a thing as simple as amusement. They'd experienced too much together for anything to feel pure.

And his love for her was worst of all.

*

When the bar closes they go back to his place, and as they're walking through the door Teresa gives him a playful look and says, 'Just because I'm coming over doesn't mean I'm gonna put out.'

'I have no expectations,' he says.

'That is the best way to avoid disappointment.'

They sit up in bed eating ice cream and watching a Humphrey Bogart film and talking about whatever it is they talk about. The conversation is a sort of free-floating entity, changing direction and shape constantly, moving from subject to subject, funny one moment and sad the next. The only consistent thing about it is that they both seem to remain lost in it.

Then, at some point soon after the ice cream is gone, they kiss.

Harry isn't sure who moved toward whom but the result is the same, and soon they are undressing one another.

Harry has always been uncomfortable during sex – it's as if a part of himself is standing outside the event, watching his every move – but this time he simply loses himself in the act, in Teresa, kissing her mouth and her neck and her breasts, stroking her cunt, then slipping himself into her as she arches her back slightly and lets out a soft moan.

And when it's over, they simply lie there, Harry breathing hard and going soft inside her, before, after what seems like several minutes, he finally rolls off and stares at the ceiling, sweating but satiated.

Teresa reaches out and takes his hand in hers.

'I'm not a whore,' she says.

'I never thought you were.'

'I just want you to know I don't do this all the time.'

'I wouldn't think less of you if you did.'

She squeezes his hand.

'Maybe,' she says. 'But I could tell you things that would make you think less of me.'

'I doubt it.'

She is silent for a very long time. He can feel her thinking, considering whether to tell him something. Then, finally, she says: 'I killed my daughter.'

'You – what?'

'It was an accident. I fell asleep with a cigarette burning and dropped it. The house caught fire. I got out with only burns on my hands. I had to grab scorching doorknobs to make it outside.' She goes silent for a moment, then: 'She didn't make it outside.'

He looks over and sees tears welling in her eyes.

'You didn't kill her. It was an accident.'

'I was a coward. I ran for safety when I should have tried to save her.'

'Everyone is a coward when their life is in danger. It's human nature.'

She shakes her head. 'I should have tried to save her.'

'You might only have gotten yourself killed.'

'Then at least I wouldn't feel this way.'

He leans over and kisses her cheek, which is wet with tears.

'That doesn't make me think less of you,' he says.

'No?'

'No. Everyone has done something they're ashamed of, something they regret.'

NOW:

1

Andrew stepped out of the motel room and walked toward his car, a duffel bag filled with last night's dirty clothes hanging from his right hand.

His father's wife walked behind him, shaking, then stopped a moment to dry heave with her bony hands resting on her knees. She was pale and sweaty and sick. Saliva hung from her mouth in a thin string before snapping and falling to the asphalt. Her appearance made her easy to dismiss, but she was more than her appearance. She was *much* more than her appearance. She was smart. She was perceptive. She had made both those things clear last night. She'd seen through him when his own father had not. But then his father had not seen through him because his father had not *wanted* to see through him.

But she could talk. He wondered how much she'd said

already, and he wondered how much of what she'd said his father believed. Certainly if she had been willing to speak to him in the way she had, she would not have remained silent with his father.

It could be the man knew what he was thinking, what he was planning, but was simply pretending he did not, for pretending would give him an advantage.

He'd have to go forward assuming his father knew more than he was letting on. If he didn't, he might underestimate the situation, and that he did not want to do, could not afford to do, not if he wanted to see Melissa again.

He threw the duffel bag into the car's backseat and slid in behind the wheel.

'Come on,' he said.

His father's wife stood up and made her way to the car, wiping her mouth with the back of a wrist. She walked as if every joint ached.

2

Though he'd not had a drop to drink the night before, Harry awoke feeling groggy and hung over and stuck half in a dream. For a moment he didn't remember why, then everything that happened last night came back to him. Everything he had done.

As did everything he had yet to do.

It was enough to make him wish his son had never tracked him down, never interrupted his peaceful little life. Then what happened last night wouldn't have happened, and what was to happen today wouldn't happen. He'd be getting up and going to the bookshop. He'd be chatting with customers about whether or not Jonathan Lethem could still be considered a science fiction writer or how great a debt he owed to Philip K. Dick or whether the latest Stephen King was his best yet or his greatest disappointment. And his son would be in Long Beach, California, living his life far away from all the death which now surrounded him. Things would be better that way, better for both of them. His son had ruined everything.

Except he didn't believe that was true, nor was it fair.

He'd dreamed for years of being reunited with his son, and if this was the price he had to pay for it happening, then so be it. It was all worth it just to get to look his son in the eyes. He was a serious young man. He was intelligent. And he appeared to be relatively stable despite the hand that Harry had dealt him. He would find trouble in his life – he already had – but if he could keep a steady head on his shoulders he would be okay. He would walk through the fire.

Harry pushed himself up, and placed his feet on the floor.

Today was going to be yet another nightmare, but with luck it would be one he lived through. That was something.

*

A cool shower helped to bring him out of his stupor. When it was over, he stepped from the tub, grabbed a towel, and dried himself off. Then he walked back to his bedroom and got dressed. He tried to think about the things he needed to do today, and he did think about them, but his brain wasn't functioning at full capacity, so he still had no idea where he would go when he left here, in what order he needed to accomplish today's tasks. He wished like hell he could take today off and rest, but now that this was begun he needed to move quickly. If the private detective got wind of what had happened last night he might go to the police, and that simply could not be allowed to happen. The man's knowledge needed to die with him, and the sooner that happened the better.

He walked upstairs to his office and opened his safe.

Once Andrew arrived he would ask the boy to make a phone call, but first there was the matter of money to deal with.

He was sitting on the couch in the living room staring at a framed print hanging on the wall when Andrew and Teresa arrived. They walked through the door, but for a moment he didn't turn to face them. He simply continued to look toward the wall. Then, after a while, he did turn to look at them.

They stood by the door. They were both looking back. Teresa appeared to be very sick.

'Good morning,' he said.

Neither of them responded.

He got to his feet and said to Andrew: 'I need you to do something.'

He drove to the convenience store with Andrew sitting beside him in the passenger seat. He didn't speak while he drove. He was thinking about what might happen once he got there, once he walked into the back room. He'd missed something the first time, had failed to see past the stockroom facade, and while that would not happen this time, he did not know what *would* happen. He thought about this, but kept his thoughts to himself.

He parked his car.

Andrew said: 'What now?'

'You wait here.'

After a moment: 'Okay.'

Harry looked at his son. The boy appeared to be very tired, his eyes haunted. Even what they'd done last night had changed him. He hadn't ended anyone's life – not yet – but he'd still been a part of two murders, and it showed. It hung on his face heavily.

But there was nothing to do about it now. One could not unexperience something.

He pushed open the driver side door and stepped out into the morning sun.

*

He pushed through the glass doors and into the fluorescent-lit convenience store. A woman in a red polyester shirt stood behind the counter. She was about forty-five, rather heavy-set, and her face was splotchy with acne.

Harry walked over to her and said: 'I need to speak to the man in back.'

She looked at him dumbly.

'Is he here?'

No response. She simply stared at him blank-eyed, chewing on bubblegum like a horse on cud. The smell was sickly sweet, the sound obnoxious.

Harry nodded. 'Okay.'

He turned away from her and toward the doorway that led to the back. When he reached it he walked through it.

On the other side he found the stockroom, and only the stockroom. He turned in a slow circle. A rectangle of bare wall moved, revealing a doorway. On the other side of the doorway was an office. And between the stockroom and the office stood a thin man with a razor-balded head and a thin John Waters mustache. He wore a well-fitting suit. One hand was in a pocket – perhaps gripping a small pistol – while the other held open the door.

'I assume you're here to see me.'

'If you're the kind of man who makes such assumptions,' Harry said, 'I'd guess you're probably right.'

'Step into my office,' the man said. 'We'll have us a little sit-down.'

*

Harry sat in a metal fold-out chair and looked across a desk to the bald man whose name he did not know. The man looked back, face placid as still water, but despite the calm Harry could tell this was a very hard man indeed – a man who felt no need to prove himself to anybody because he'd done all the proving he'd needed to long ago. He was a man who did what he had to when he had to, who did it without hesitation, but was otherwise content to remain still. Such men, in Harry's experience, were very dangerous.

Harry liked him immediately.

'Why are you here?'

'My name is Harry White.'

The man nodded. 'I know who you are. Why are you here?'

'You sent two men to my house last night.'

'I did, and I've not seen them since.'

'You won't.'

A smile briefly touched the man's lips and shone behind his eyes, but also a touch of anger. 'Those were two of my best men.'

'You should get better men.'

'It's a poor workforce these days.'

'Better wages might remedy that.'

'The pay is ample. Are you applying?'

'I'm a broken-down old man.'

'And yet you've disappeared two of my best.'

Harry shrugged. 'Luck, I guess.'

'I doubt that very much.'

'We'll call it luck.'

'Why are you here?'

Harry pulled two bundles of cash from his pockets, leaned forward, and set them on the desk one atop the other.

'What's this?'

'Twenty thousand dollars.'

'Why is it on my desk?'

'To pay Silas Green's debt, plus a little more.'

'I must admit to being confused.'

'About what?'

'Why do what you did last night only to come here with the money I was trying to obtain? You could have just paid my men.'

'I won't be pushed. That doesn't mean we can't come to terms.'

'What terms?'

'I'm here because he's mine. Because I have a small business in town. Because I don't want any more trouble from you or any of your employees. But mostly because he's mine. Silas Green belongs to me. If his debt is paid that takes you out of the equation.'

'Fair enough. Silas Green's debt is now paid in full.'

'Would you mind also giving him a call and letting him know that his situation has been dealt with?'

'Now you're asking favors?'

'For old times' sake.'

The man nodded.

'Thank you.'

He got to his feet and turned toward the door.

'Just one thing.'

Harry looked back at the man behind the desk.

'What did he do to you?'

Harry didn't answer for a long time. Then: 'He simply made the mistake of assuming that because I'm a quiet man I'm also a peaceful one – and he should have known better.'

The man nodded. 'I understand.'

'I'm sure you do.'

Harry stepped through the door.

3

Andrew watched as his father stepped from the convenience store and walked toward the car. He grabbed the handle, pulled open the door, fell in behind the wheel. He put his head against the wheel and closed his eyes. He exhaled.

'Did it go all right?'

His father sat up and looked at him. 'It couldn't have gone any better.' His tone was dry, sounded almost sarcastic, but Andrew had a feeling he meant exactly what he said.

'What's next?'

'We take care of Silas Green.'

With those words Andrew went numb inside. This was it then. This was his big test. This was when he found out if he had what it took to do what he had to do, and he was suddenly very afraid he didn't. He was suddenly certain he didn't. He would not be able to follow through. He would not be able to finish the man, and if he couldn't do that he certainly couldn't do his father, for he felt nothing at all for Silas Green while for his father he felt love and hatred, respect and contempt, admiration and pity, and those were complicated feelings to push aside for math.

'Andrew?'

He looked at his father.

'Are you okay?'

Andrew nodded.

4

While Harry drove he thought about the pistol in his glove box. It had once belonged to a man who now lay at the bottom of the Ohio River. If they could draw Silas Green close enough it would work well to finish him. And they *could* draw him close enough. The man was about to learn that Harry Combs was dead, which meant his guard was about to fall, which meant the phone call Andrew had made this morning should easily pull him in. If Harry Combs were alive, Silas Green might be very cautious.

Harry Combs, however, was not still alive. But there was another question which would affect the outcome. Could Andrew follow through and do the job he said he wanted to do? Harry simply didn't know. The boy was sitting still and silent beside him, but Harry could tell that inside he was a nervous wreck.

Yet Harry almost hoped the boy wouldn't be able to follow through. It would mean that he'd have to clean up the mess himself, but it would also mean that Andrew was not a killer, and he didn't want for Andrew what he had had. He knew what it did to a man to take the life of another. He knew how it hardened one's heart, like that Pharaoh in the bible, and how that hardening affected all aspects of one's existence.

He'd happily clean up the mess if it meant that his son could remain innocent. He was already the man he was, after all, despite how he'd tried to be someone else. When it came time to do what needed doing he'd not hesitated. Harry Combs was there and he was ready. Harry White was mere smoke hiding the reality that lay behind, and when he should have remained firm he'd broken apart on the wind.

Harry White would not have threatened anybody, cut anybody, killed anybody.

But Harry Combs would – and did.

He parked the car on the street in front of Teresa's small rental house.

'This is where it's going to be done.'

'Why here?'

'You can do it inside and I'll have a chance to take care of the mess. We get rid of the body, there will be nothing to explain. And no one will ever think to look here anyway once we take care of the office and anything that might lead police here.'

'How am I going to do this?'

Harry looked at his son and saw that the boy was actually asking two questions. He wanted to know both what actions he should take to do the job and what he had to do internally in order that he might be capable of them.

'Does he know your face?'

'No.'

'I didn't think so. Because of the phone call you made this morning he'll be here at eleven thirty to discuss a very personal matter. Get him inside, offer him something to drink. It's okay if you seem nervous. He'll be used to that. He'll sit down and let you take your time. You'll go into the kitchen to get his drink. When you return you'll shoot him. Do it three times, once in the head and twice in the chest. Go for the chest first. It's an easier target, a bigger target. Do it quickly and don't miss.'

Andrew nodded. 'Okay.'

Harry was silent for a long time. He simply sat looking at the expression on his son's face. Finally he said: 'You don't have to do this.'

'I do.'

'You don't.'

'I *do*. I do have to do this.'

'You're sure?'

'Yes.'

'Okay. There's a gun in the glove box.'

Andrew opened it and pulled out the pistol. He held it in both hands, examining both it and the attached silencer. He held it as if it were an alien object, some artifact from another planet. This was not good, not good at all, but things had already been set in motion and there was no going back. They didn't have time to go back. This needed to be finished.

'Get close to him before you pull the trigger.'

Andrew looked up. 'How close?'

'It's best if you're within ten feet of him.'

'Okay.'

'You sure you're up to this?'

Andrew swallowed. 'I have to be.'

5

Andrew sat in the house for what seemed like a very long time. He felt sick to his stomach, unsure of himself. He wondered how he'd let things get this far and couldn't figure it out. For years he'd had fantasies of killing his father, of avenging his mother's death, but this was something else altogether. This was *real*, and reality was a terrible thing. It was so goddamn unbelievably *final*.

And yet there was something in him that also needed this done. He felt it tight in his chest, felt it squeezing down on his heart, gripping it like a fist, and he knew there was but one way to relieve that terrible pressure. His whole life he'd felt it, but never more than now, and there was only one thing he could do to be free of it.

He wanted to cry.

He wanted to go home and put his head in Melissa's lap.

He wanted his father dead.

This was going to change him. His father was right about that. He could feel it even now as he tried to steel himself for it. He was very likely going to become something he despised. He wanted to back out of it. He wanted desperately to back out of it. But he could not, and he didn't know why. When he thought about what he might become – what he *would* become – he knew that doing this would not really solve anything. He *knew* it. And yet there was something else in him that demanded it be done anyway, and that something else was stronger than his brain, stronger than anything else within him. It had to be done.

It absolutely *had* to be done.

There was no way around it.

6

Harry sat in his car watching the private detective's office. He'd smoked half a pack of cigarettes while sitting here in this parking lot across the street from the man whose life Andrew was to take. He was nervous, much more nervous than he'd be were he to do the job himself. His head would not be filled with any of the questions with which it was now swimming. His mind would be silent as an empty room. His body would be a machine. It would happen and it would be over and he'd clean up the mess as one would clean a beer dropped on a tile floor.

Silas Green stepped through his glass door.

Harry turned the key in his ignition. The engine roared to life.

The private detective got into his car. A moment later it backed out of its parking spot, then rolled toward the driveway and out into the street.

Harry put his own car into gear and pulled out behind him.

He didn't want his son to do this but knew that at this point he could not question it. It was happening, and it would be best if it all went down as smoothly as possible. If Andrew's aim was not true and the man died slowly, writhed in pain, or tried to defend himself his son would not react well. He knew it absolutely.

It had to happen fast and it had to happen easy.

But just in case it didn't, Harry would be there.

7

A car pulled to a stop in the driveway. The engine died. Andrew stood up, sat down, stood up again. He thought about the gun in the kitchen. He thought about pulling the trigger, ending this man's life. He didn't know if he could do it. All the times he'd imagined it were meaningless. All those waking dreams proved nothing. What mattered was what he did here today. If he couldn't do this he might as well pack up and drive home. He would still hold within him that terrible pressure, he'd still want to erase his father, but he'd know finally that he was incapable of such an action, and maybe that knowledge would provide some sort of—

A knock at the door.

Andrew walks to it calmly, grabs the doorknob, feels nothing.

A knock at the door.

Andrew walked to it nervously, grabbed the doorknob. He was filled with turmoil. He was filled with dread and with doubt. His stomach was a fist-sized cramp threatening to bend him over. He was sweaty and sick.

He looks at the man and sees no man at all, merely an obstacle, something to get out of the way before moving forward.

He looked at the man, at the light in his eyes, and thought about how the man's mother would react when she received the news. Her face would contort with agony. A bestial wail might escape her throat, nearly forming words but not quite, oh God, no. She'd think of him as a baby, his tongue pulling at her nipple. She'd think of him as a boy playing catch. She'd think of him as a young man coming home for the holidays.

And Andrew thought of the man as well. All his dreams were about to be snuffed out. If he could do this the man would simply cease to exist. The matter that made him up would still be present, of course, but the man himself would be gone, simply erased like a pencil smudge on a sheet of paper, leaving behind only blank white nothing.

'Hello,' Andrew said.

'Silas Green.' The private detective put out his hand.

Andrew shook it. It was warm, but soon it would be cold. Soon the nerves within it would feel nothing, respond to nothing. It was strange to think about in those terms. What turned certain collections of matter into living things? What ethereal quality was removed when a living thing died? He didn't know. He couldn't know – not now, not ever – maybe no one could, and yet he was playing with life and death.

With death, anyway.

'Come on in,' he said.

The private detective stepped into the house. Andrew

closed the door behind him. He looked at the man, looked at his eyes and his mouth and the gauze bandage covering his cheek. Soon, if he could do this, the man would be incapable of looking back.

'Would you like something to drink?'

'I could do with some bourbon,' the private detective said, then laughed. 'A glass of water would be fine.'

Andrew nodded. 'Okay. Have a seat.'

The only place to sit was a dirty couch the previous tenants had apparently left behind. All other furniture was absent.

'Spartan arrangement you got here.'

'I – I like things simple.'

'I can understand that. Things do tend to get compli- cated quickly.'

'Let me – let me get your water.'

Andrew turned, his body feeling as though it was moving very unnaturally – everything felt stiff and awk- ward – and walked jerkily toward the kitchen.

This was it.

8

Harry parked on the street half a block from the house and stepped out of his vehicle. He lit a cigarette, walked around to the back of his car. He popped the trunk and from within removed his chopped baseball bat. There was still blood on it from last night's trouble. With luck Andrew would be able to take care of the private detective himself, but it was never wise to count on luck. It was a simple fact that whenever you did, luck got a flat on the interstate and ended up not showing.

He walked along the sidewalk to the narrow white-painted house and wondered what was happening within it. He wondered too what was going through Andrew's head. Killing a man for the first time is not what you expect it to be. Even if you're able to do it, even if you're able to justify it to yourself in a logical manner – all emotion removed from your considerations – even then it is very different from what you expect it to be, for murder is a primitive act, and from the moment we're born we are trained to be civilized. We say please and thank you and make certain we're using the correct fork. But murder taps into a different part of us, a part that we usually keep hidden in darkness, even from ourselves. Occasionally even the nicest people, the kindest of men, will experience the most violent mental lightning – someone cuts them off in traffic and a flash of rage ignites their mind, and murderous electricity briefly courses through their veins – but one knows better than to act on such things. One remains grounded. The electricity flows safely into the earth, and order remains undisturbed.

Yes, mostly that's how it goes.

But not always.

And those who have killed know the power of murder.

They know that the part of them capable of it is in many ways more *real* than the part of them which makes certain not to double-dip their celery stick at a gathering. That part of them is facade. But there is nothing fake about killing a man. It is terrible. It is often unforgivable. But it is also very, very real.

Andrew was about to find out how real. He was about to give over control to a part of himself most men never access, and once that happens one was changed. Once that storm center was fed with violence it grew stronger, and the lightning became more frequent. Often it became overpowering.

You can suppress it – sometimes for years – but you can never kill it.

Even after twenty-six years in the basement of his soul that part of him was present. And it was as strong as ever.

He walked up three concrete steps to the front porch.

He stood by the door, listening.

He waited.

9

Andrew walked to the cupboard and pulled it open. On an otherwise empty shelf lay the pistol with which he was supposed to murder the private detective. He wrapped his hand around the grip and pulled it from the shelf, the silencer dragging heavily against the wood surface. He closed his eyes as it left the shelf and its weight came to be supported only by his right hand.

He shuts himself off, closes himself down one compartment after another, until all feeling is locked away and what he's left with is mere thought, and his only thought is to get this done, get this over with so he can move on.

He opens his eyes and turns toward the living room.

For a moment he doesn't move, then he does move. He takes a step. The first is followed by others, each one carrying him closer to the man he is supposed to kill.

He steps into the living room.

'I don't have any water,' he says.

Andrew blinked and found himself looking at the private detective. It was a surprise to find himself here in the living room, to find himself looking at the man he was supposed to kill. Until this moment he'd believed himself to be in the kitchen, but here he was, and he realized too that the words he'd imagined had actually left his mouth.

His heart began pounding in his chest.

He felt disoriented.

That was supposed to be mere fantasy.

The private detective looked from Andrew's eyes to his hand and the gun gripped within it. His face contorted with emotion and he seemed to climb up the couch on which he was sitting in order to get away from Andrew.

Andrew raised the pistol. He had to act. He had to act now. This was it. It was happening. He wasn't ready for it but he was here and it was happening.

He squeezed the trigger.

The private detective grunted and dropped back into the couch. His shoulder was bleeding. Tears were streaming down his face. He looked confused and frightened. He looked like a little boy. He was not a cow. He was not merely animated meat. He was a man and he was scared.

'Why are you doing—'

Andrew squeezed the trigger again and the man's mouth seemed to explode, teeth scattering across the room and blood spattering the walls.

The private detective put his hand over his mouth.

Blood flowed out between his fingers.

He worked to his feet.

'Please,' he tried to say, but it came out garbled and somehow *wet*. He pushed himself to his feet, almost falling down but managing to maintain his balance. He walked toward Andrew with a pleading hand outstretched. It was covered in blood from his mouth. Tears continued to stream down his cheeks. Blood poured from his mouth, down his chin, dripping onto his chest.

Andrew began to shake and the gun shook with him.

He squeezed the trigger a third time, but missed, the bullet imbedding itself in the wall.

His fourth shot missed as well.

The private detective grabbed his wrist and despite himself Andrew let out a scream and flinched back. He dropped the gun. It thudded to the floor.

He looked down at it and thought to pick it up, but he felt frozen in place.

He looked back up at the private detective.

'Please,' the man said again – or tried to. 'Please.'

10

Harry heard Andrew scream, heard the gun drop to the floor, and with those sounds knew it was time to take action. He pushed into the room and quickly assessed the situation. Andrew and the private detective were standing close enough to kiss, the private detective holding Andrew's wrist. The gun lay on the floor between their feet. Blood poured from the private detective's mouth and flecks of shattered tooth clung to his chin with a glue of saliva and blood.

Harry took three quick steps and swung the baseball bat. It thudded hard against the side of the private detective's skull.

The man fell to his knees.

Harry hit him again, and again, and again. He hit the back of the skull until the hard surface became soft, until the bone was broken into small shards and he was bashing soft tissue, until it felt like he was hitting a sack of oatmeal.

Finally he stopped.

He got to his feet. His arm was sore, his shoulder throbbing.

He looked at Andrew. Andrew looked back horrified, eyes wide and mouth agape.

'It had to be done,' Harry said.

Andrew did not respond.

'I had to finish what you started.'

Finally, after what felt to Harry like a very long time, Andrew nodded. 'I – I know,' he said. Then: 'I'm gonna – I'm going to wait outside.'

He turned and walked jerkily toward the front door.

THEN:

Too impatient to wait on the draft Harry joins the army at eighteen, joins the day after he graduates high school, not because of any special sense of patriotism – patriotism in the traditional sense is something he doesn't and has never under-stood: being proud of one's country seems nonsensical; it is a thing for which one bears no responsibility, and if one is not responsible for something, how can one be proud of it? – but because he wants to get out of his parents' house and he is young enough and stupid enough to believe life in the army will be an adventure. He thinks of old men he's heard talking about their time in the First World War, and he expects he'll have tales such as theirs. He expects that one day he too will be an interesting old man hunched over his beer at a bar telling tales of killing the enemy and fucking foreign women from whom he contracted terrible venereal diseases, but boy was it worth it, you should have seen this broad.

It is summer 1944, and he's all but certain he'll be shipped off to Germany in a matter of weeks. He hopes he is. The further he can get from Orange County the better; the further he can get from his parents the better.

He walks into the recruiting office, a two-hundred-square-foot room with three desks in it, the walls lined with army posters – and tells the first person in uniform he sees that he'd like to sign up, that he'd like to go to war. The man smiles – somewhat condescendingly, his smile seeming to say you don't know what war is – and walks Harry to another uniformed man sitting behind a small oak desk.

'We got us a soldier,' the first man says.

'Always good to meet a young man with direction. Have a seat.'

If he knew what this would lead to – if he knew that his calm nerves and his sure shot would make him a valuable killer to the United States government, if he knew what being such a man would do to his soul – he would walk back out into the southern California sun.

But as with his letter twenty years later, he does not and cannot know.

So he sits down across from the man at the desk and he signs his life away.

NOW:

1

Andrew was standing on the front porch with his hands in his pockets. He was thinking about what happened inside – and what didn't happen. What didn't happen was him killing Silas Green. What didn't happen was him confirming he could do what he needed to do. What didn't happen was him proving himself *to* himself. He had pulled the trigger but he had failed all the same. His nerves had failed him. His heart had failed him.

He had failed himself.

Before going into this he had been so certain that he'd be capable of turning himself off and of handling the situation coolly. But once he was in the middle of it he'd found there was nothing cool about him. He was a mess and the killing was a disaster. It was no killing at all. It was a maiming.

Until his father arrived, anyway.

That had been when he'd *really* seen the difference between them.

His father might be warm, might be loving, might be gentle, but there was also a corner of his heart that was very black indeed. What he'd done in there without hesitation and without apparent emotional involvement had been absolutely brutal, and absolutely shocking in its brutality. If his father had displayed any emotion at all it would have at least felt like a human act – a terrible act to be sure, but a *human* one – but he'd displayed nothing but cold detachment and violence.

Andrew could never do that.

As angry as he was, as full of hatred as he was, he could *never* do that.

And yet – and yet even knowing this to be true he wanted to kill the man. He wanted to kill him in anger, wanted to kill him in rage, wanted to smother him in his hatred until he was finally dead.

To hell with algebra.

His reason for murder was not of the mind; it was a reason of the heart. And he was convinced that if you were going to kill for such a reason you should let your heart *feel* it. His father had been trying to teach him to assassinate someone, but what he needed to do was not an assassination. It was a murder. He'd confused them himself for a while, but they were very different things, and algebra had about as much to do with the latter as spiders had to do with wedding cake.

It was true that he had failed today, but he'd failed not because he had not been able to remain cool and calm but because he had attempted it at all. He should not even have tried to kill Silas Green, for the private detective was not the man he wanted. He had been wrong to think of it as a test. He had been wrong to think he could learn to murder. The emotional landscape was so different from the one he was walking into that it told him nothing at all about what he'd feel when he gazed upon his father's sunset.

And he did still intend to put a gun to his father's head.

Not coolly, not while feeling detached, but with a head and heart full of rage and hatred and resentment. He intended to unleash it all so that he might finally be free of it. If he tried to fight his feelings as he'd done today he would be unable to pull the trigger, for it was those feelings which would finally push him forward.

Yes – he knew now that that was how it had to be done, and he fully intended to do it, and in doing it in that way he would not become his father. He *could* not become his father. There was no chance of that at all, for his actions would be driven by something else altogether. His father was cold while he was burning up.

So no, he would not become his father. He would simply become free of him.

2

Harry looked at the mess and thought about his son. The boy had fucked up. It was something Harry had hoped wouldn't happen, but now that it had he was almost glad of it. Had it gone smoothly, had it gone well, his son might not fully understand what he'd done. But he understood this. That much was clear by how deeply it had affected him. It was also clear by the *way* it had affected him. Harry had reacted to his first kill differently. It was true that his had been in the midst of a just war – perhaps the *last* just war – but still: he'd felt a rush when his man went down. Look what I have accomplished with my calm nerves and my trigger finger: an erasure of the highest order.

It was clear his son felt no such thing. Simple horror had been written across his face and nothing more.

So now it was done – and now the boy knew.

Harry rolled the private detective over with his foot. His face was recognizable, but the river and time would take care of that. His teeth were Harry's concern, and while several had been taken care of already, there were at least another fifteen that could be used for identification purposes. Harry gripped the bat in his hand, sighed, and swung down hard. He heard the jaw break. The head turned hard. Several teeth fell from the open mouth.

It was a start.

3

His father disposed of the body in the river. Andrew watched from the rocks as the old man dragged the loaded and tied tarp toward the water and then rolled the bundle into it. He watched as it knocked against a rock and was carried away by the current. He watched as it floated down the river, dipping under, disappearing more and more frequently before finally vanishing into the murk and froth completely.

His father turned and their eyes locked.

He stood there on the shore in a cardigan sweater and khaki pants, his gray hair tousled, his face looking old and tired. His shoulders were slumped with age. His eyes were large and warm, the eyes of your favorite grade-school teacher.

He was the most coldly violent man Andrew had ever encountered.

4

Harry got into the private detective's Honda Prelude. It smelled of cheap cologne and cigar smoke. He turned the key in the ignition with a gloved hand and the engine came to life in a series of fits and starts. He put the transmission into gear and backed out of his parking spot. They had but one more job to do before they were finally finished with this mess, and the sooner they were done with it the better.

He unlocked the door of the private detective's office and stepped inside. A desk sat in the middle of the square room. On top of the desk rested a telephone, an electric typewriter, and several stacks of papers both hand- and typewritten. Against the side wall sat two wooden chairs with cushioned seats and a small rectangular table with a few magazines fanned across its surface. The room seemed very stark in its lack of humanness. The desk was bare of even the slightest personal touch, the walls were bare of pictures – even pictures of the mass-produced variety – and not even a *dead* plant ornamented one of the corners.

Harry walked to the desk and began flipping through the paperwork.

It took him thirty minutes to go through both what was visible on the desk's surface and what was hidden away in a file drawer, but when he was done he'd found pictures of himself, a carbon copy of a short typewritten report, a handwritten note about today's appointment, and a carbon copy of correspondence between Silas Green and a private detective in California named Francis Martin, presumably the man Andrew had originally employed to find him.

After going through all he'd gone through he was faced with the possibility that there was a man in California who might cause trouble for him. It put a cramp into his stomach. But it wasn't something he could think about right now, wasn't something he could worry about. The man had thus far been harmless. He might simply be a man who took his assignments and asked no further questions. His complete lack of presence suggested he was exactly that. For now Harry would forget him. If he heard his name even one more time, in any context, he might begin to worry about him, but for now he'd deal with the problem in front of him.

He folded the paperwork in half lengthwise and slipped it into his back pocket before venturing down the hall to a back room which contained a Xerox machine and several metal file cabinets. He sighed looking at them all, but knew he had to be thorough.

If the private detective's body never turned up, or was never identified, he'd simply be a missing person forever. But even missing persons received a fair amount of attention from the police and Harry did not want them to come across anything which might make them aware of his existence. It was important that the police never even see him in their periphery. If they did, they might turn their heads to get a better look, and who knew what they'd see if they did that?

He walked to the first file cabinet and pulled open the top drawer.

5

Andrew sat behind the wheel of his father's car and waited for him to return from his task. He looked down at his wrist and saw that blood had dried there. He scratched at it with a fingernail and it flaked away. The blood had once belonged to a man named Silas Green. Now it belonged to nobody. The man who'd once claimed it existed no more. That was a strange thing to think about and a hard thing to believe. Wasn't his body even now floating down the river or lying at its bottom? It was. And if his body was there, if his body still existed in the world but he no longer inhabited it, where the hell had the man himself gone?

Probably he had simply been snuffed out like a candle flame. And where did flames go when they stopped burning? They went nowhere.

They simply ceased to exist while the candle remained.

There was no heaven for fire. But was there one for men? He didn't know.

As a small boy he'd believed there was. He'd been *certain* of it. And while he was much less certain now, a very large part of him wanted to believe.

But if there was a heaven, didn't that mean his father had committed no crime? He'd committed one in the eyes of man, of course, but in the eyes of God? His father had merely spent his time driving people home. They'd only been tourists here, after all, taking their holidays on earth like the rest of us. God must have approved of his father's actions or he would not have permitted them. That was what it meant to be omnipotent. If you didn't like something you stopped it, and if you allowed something to happen that you *could* have stopped you were giving that something your silent approval.

That would also mean that today *he* had done God's work. So there was no reason to feel what he was feeling. He liked that. He liked it because the more he thought about what had happened today – what he'd done – the worse he felt. The shock of it was melting away. What was left behind was an ugly core of guilt and regret.

What had he been thinking? Why had he believed he should kill a man who had never wronged him? Why had he pulled the trigger when he'd felt like he had? Shouldn't what he'd felt have been enough to let him know he was not meant to go forward? How could he believe he had the right to erase someone's existence? His hopes, dreams, and future?

But perhaps simply doing the thing had proved he had the right. If he hadn't then God would not have allowed it.

There was something wonderfully calming about that thought and he tried to believe it. He tried but could not sustain it. For if his father was blameless, then he had no right to hate the man – he had no right to feel this rage within him, no right to kill his father for his crimes – and there was simply no way that he'd let God take that away from him. His heart demanded vengeance, and he would have it. And if he was to justify it to himself, he had to believe his father had done wrong, and he did believe it.

If that meant he also had to own what he'd done today then so be it. He would own it. He would own it in order that his father also own *his* crimes. The man was brutal and cold and violent. He had killed his own wife, abandoned his son. He would pay for those things and he would pay for them with his life.

Andrew would simply have to live with what he'd done.

6

Harry stepped out of the office building and locked the door behind him. He was now certain that not a single sheet of paper mentioning either Harry Combs or Harry White existed within that building. It was clean. The paperwork he'd found he would take home and burn. In a few days someone would notice that Silas Green hadn't been around. Eventually the police would start searching for him. But he had no connection to the man. There was no reason for him to ever come to anyone's attention.

He walked to Silas Green's Honda Prelude and put the keys into the ignition. He'd been wearing gloves at every point he'd come in contact with it, so there was no need to wipe the thing down for prints. He locked the door and slammed it shut. He looked at it for a long moment, then turned toward his own vehicle. His son was sitting behind the wheel watching him. The look on his face was not a pleasant one, though he doubted very much his son was even aware of his expression.

Teresa was right. There was something wrong with the boy. There was something very bad living inside him, something dangerous. It was in his eyes. It was even in his posture. Some bad seed had been planted inside him, and now it was growing, spreading its vines into his heart and mind, taking over completely.

Harry walked to the car and pulled open the passenger door. He got inside.

'You know how to get home from here?'

His son nodded.

Harry fastened his seatbelt. 'Okay.'

Andrew turned the key in the ignition and the engine roared to life. He put the car into reverse and backed out of the parking spot.

Harry thought of that look on his face. Murder had been written across it and hatred – deep hatred. The boy was well beyond angry. He was sick. He'd been contaminated by bad emotions. How Harry'd not seen that before now was a mystery, but he hadn't. Perhaps what happened today with the private detective had brought it out of the boy in some way. He didn't know. What he did know was that the hatred was there and had been all along. He'd simply have to wait and see what the boy intended to do about it. He hoped nothing drastic. It would be terrible after all these years to finally meet his son as a man and for it to go completely sideways. All he wanted was to have some kind of relationship with the boy. All he wanted was to be allowed to love him. But he didn't think that would ever happen.

What he didn't know was what *would* happen.

Excerpt from 'A Study of Assassination', a CIA pamphlet distributed to agents

Techniques for assassination are as follows:

1. Manual.
It is possible to kill a man with the bare hands, but very few are skillful enough to do it well. Even a highly trained Judo expert will hesitate to risk killing by hand unless he has absolutely no alternative.

However, the simplest local tools are often the most efficient means of assassination. A hammer, axe, wrench, screw driver, fire poker, kitchen knife, lamp stand, or anything hard, heavy and handy will suffice. A length of rope or wire or a belt will do if the assassin is strong and agile. All such improvised weapons have the important advantage of availability and apparent innocence. The obviously lethal machine gun failed to kill Trotsky where an item of sporting goods succeeded.

In all safe cases where the assassin may be subject to

search, either before or after the act, specialized weapons should not be used. Even in the lost case, the assassin may accidentally be searched before the act and should not carry an incriminating device if any sort of lethal weapon can be improvised at or near the site. If the assassin normally carries weapons because of the nature of his job, it may still be desirable to improvise and implement at the scene to avoid disclosure of his identity.

2. Accidents.

For secret assassination, either simple or chase, the contrived accident is the most effective technique. When successfully executed, it causes little excitement and is only casually investigated.

The most efficient accident, in simple assassination, is a fall of 75 feet or more onto a hard surface. Elevator shafts, stair wells, unscreened windows and bridges will serve. Bridge falls into water are not reliable. In simple cases a private meeting with the subject may be arranged at a properly cased location. The act may be executed by sudden, vigorous [excised] of the ankles, tipping the subject over the edge. If the assassin immediately sets up an outcry, playing the 'horrified witness', no alibi or surreptitious withdrawal is necessary. In chase cases it will usually be necessary to stun or drug the subject before dropping him. Care is required to ensure that no wound or condition not attributable to the fall is discernible after death.

Falls into the sea or swiftly flowing rivers may suffice if

the subject cannot swim. It will be more reliable if the assassin can arrange to attempt rescue, as he can thus be sure of the subject's death and at the same time establish a workable alibi.

If the subject's personal habits make it feasible, alcohol may be used to prepare him for a contrived accident of any kind. Falls before trains or subway cars are usually effective, but require exact timing and can seldom be free from unexpected observation.

Automobile accidents are a less satisfactory means of assassination. If the subject is deliberately run down, very exact timing is necessary and investigation is likely to be thorough. If the subject's car is tampered with, reliability is very low. The subject may be stunned or drugged and then placed in the car, but this is only reliable when the car can be run off a high cliff or into deep water without observation.

Arson can cause accidental death if the subject is drugged and left in a burning building. Reliability is not satisfactory unless the building is isolated and highly combustible.

3. Drugs.
In all types of assassination except terroristic, drugs can be very effective. If the assassin is trained as a doctor or nurse and the subject is under medical care, this is an easy and rare method. An overdose of morphine administered as

a sedative will cause death without disturbance and is difficult to detect.

The size of the dose will depend upon whether the subject has been using narcotics regularly. If not, two grains will suffice. If the subject drinks heavily, morphine or a similar narcotic can be injected at the passing out stage, and the cause of death will often be held to be acute alcoholism.

Specific poisons, such as arsenic or strychnine, are effective but their possession or procurement is incriminating, and accurate dosage is problematical. Poison was used unsuccessfully in the assassination of Rasputin and Kolohan, though the latter case is more accurately described as a murder.

4. Edge Weapons.

Any locally obtained edge device may be successfully employed. A certain minimum of anatomical knowledge is needed for reliability.

Puncture wounds of the body cavity may not be reliable unless the heart is reached. The heart is protected by the rib cage and is not always easy to locate.

Abdominal wounds were once nearly always mortal, but modern medical treatment has made this no longer true.

Absolute reliability is obtained by severing the spinal cord in the cervical region. This can be done with the point of a knife or a light blow of an axe or hatchet.

Another reliable method is the severing of both jugular and carotid blood vessels on both sides of the windpipe.

If the subject has been rendered unconscious by other wounds or drugs, either of the above methods can be used to ensure death.

5. Blunt Weapons.

As with edge weapons, blunt weapons require some anatomical knowledge for effective use. Their main advantage is their universal availability. A hammer may be picked up almost anywhere in the world. Baseball bats are very widely distributed. Even a rock or a heavy stick will do, and nothing resembling a weapon need be procured, carried or subsequently disposed of.

Blows should be directed to the temple, the area just below and behind the ear, and the lower, rear portion of the skull. Of course, if the blow is very heavy, any portion of the upper skull will do. The lower frontal portion of the head, from the eyes to the throat, can withstand enormous blows without fatal consequences.

PART THREE

A GOOD MAN

Every man is the son of his own works.
Cervantes

THEN:

Harry's involvement in organized crime begins when he is twenty-three. He's been out of the army over two years and, because of a botched job for the CIA, has not had a government contract in over six months. In that time he has been walking around in an angry haze. Despite leaving the war over two years ago, it has not yet left him. It hovers around him constantly like his own personal weather system, perhaps because until now he's not had time to sit still and consider it. All of these suppressed moments have blown back to the front of his mind.

He's been staying in Dallas, sleeping on an old army buddy's couch despite the man's wife being furious that he's there – you told me he'd be here a few days; *it's been* months – *but he must stay for now as he's been unable to find work. There are plenty of people willing to call him a hero while not hiring him, of course (words cost them not a goddamn thing), but there aren't any willing to provide him with a steady paycheck. It* seems his skillset is not exactly marketable in the civilian world.

He's talking about this in a bar with his buddy when a suited man two stools down leans over and says: 'What exactly is your skillset?'

Harry doesn't say anything for a long time. He doesn't know how to answer. Then he decides on blunt honesty: 'I know how to kill people.'

'Let me buy you a drink,' the man says.

NOW:

1

Andrew awakened the next day at half past eight and lay in bed for another twenty minutes staring at the ceiling. He awoke knowing what he was going to say to his father, what he hoped he and his father would do about it. He thought it likely to go the way he hoped – particularly since his father had already begun down that road – and if his father reacted in the way Andrew hoped he did, then Andrew could take care of him without worrying about the police. They would make assumptions about the man's death that would eliminate Andrew before he could even be implicated. They'd identify the body, discover who he'd been, and, because of where he was, put together the wrong pieces in just the right way. Their investigation would be perfunctory at best, since they'd go into it knowing what had happened – thinking they knew what happened, anyway.

That was his hope.

He got out of bed and slipped into clean clothes, pulling them from the suitcase on the floor. His father had already burned the bloody things he had on yesterday in the small fire pit in his backyard. He was glad to be rid of them – not for evidentiary reasons but because he didn't want to be reminded of what had happened every time he slipped into them. He didn't want to see the private detective's face, the flecks of teeth sticking to his chin. He didn't want to smell the gunpowder in the air.

He stepped out of the bedroom and into the hallway, then walked to the kitchen. His father was sitting at the table with Teresa. They were both drinking coffee. Teresa looked much better. She was still too thin, and pale, and there were dark circles under her eyes, but she also appeared to be lucid and looked almost healthy. And almost happy – until she saw him in the kitchen doorway and her face changed. Her eyebrows lowered in the middle and her lips went tight. Then she looked back toward her husband without even so much as a g'mornin and took a sip of her coffee.

Her feelings were clear. He was not worth her time.

Andrew looked at the clock on the stove and said: 'You should have woken me up. I didn't realize it was so late.'

His father turned around and looked at him. 'You needed the sleep.'

Andrew nodded. 'I did.'

'How do you feel?'

'Much better.'

'Feel like doing a little fishing today?'

'Fishing?'

'Give us a chance to relax and talk.'

'We could do that.'

'Then it's a plan. Why don't you get a shower and we'll head out in half an hour or so?'

Andrew nodded. 'Okay.'

2

Harry watched Andrew walk out of the kitchen. Then he turned toward Teresa. She was looking at him intently, examining his face, reading his emotional state in a way she hadn't done in years. It made him feel self-conscious but he also liked it. It made him feel connected to her. He'd missed that very much. For years they had seemed simply to coexist, filling their roles in life without thought or emotional engagement. Since Andrew's arrival, though, things had changed. He wasn't sure why or how, but he knew that they had.

'You see it now, don't you?'

'See what?'

'That something is wrong with Andrew.'

Harry nodded. 'But whatever is wrong with him is wrong with me too.'

'You don't have hate in you, not like that.'

'I'm not sure *why* someone does something matters as much as *what* that someone does, and in that regard he's the better person.'

'You're the better person. Everything you've had to deal with lately – I know you won't tell me about it, but I'm not blind – everything you've had to deal with lately is a direct result of his actions, of his coming here. He's brought out the worst in you. I know that. I've seen the man you were before we met. But people deserve to be measured by what's best in them, not what's worst.'

'Shouldn't that extend to Andrew?'

'Not when he's a threat to the man I love.'

'He's not a threat.'

'Why do you say that?'

'What do you mean?'

'If you're telling me he isn't a threat because you can handle him I trust you, but if you think he's *really* not a threat I say you're blind.'

'I can handle him.'

Teresa didn't respond for a long time, just looked into his eyes. Then, finally, she nodded and said: 'Okay.' Harry wasn't certain she believed him, but she said it, and that was enough. It meant she would require no more of him. It meant she would let the conversation stop there.

'Okay,' he said. He took a sip of his coffee, looked down into the pool of dark liquid contained within his mug. He could see his own distorted reflection in it.

What he'd said to Teresa was not a lie, but it was

hardly the truth either. He *could* handle Andrew if it came to that – the boy could not get to him if he didn't allow it to happen – but he wasn't at all certain he would. If Andrew hated him enough to kill him he might well allow it to happen, for he could not stand the thought of being hated by the boy, and he could not stand the thought of doing what would be necessary to stop him.

He was already responsible for the death of his first wife, and because of that he had brought his son's hatred upon himself. He had *earned* it.

That being true, perhaps he also deserved to be killed.

The math certainly seemed to suggest it. So if his son wanted him dead, if he could not make his son believe that he was worthy of breath, perhaps he would simply allow the boy to make the subtraction he wanted to make.

His only real regret would be leaving Teresa behind. He was not at all certain she would make it without him, and he was not at all certain he should sacrifice a twenty-two-year marriage for a young man he barely knew.

Andrew was his son, that was true, and he'd earned his son's hatred sure, but Teresa had earned neither that nor abandonment. She had loved him wholly, faults and all, and she deserved to have him here to love, and to be loved by him.

And yet – and yet there was a part of Harry that wanted to let it all go. He was exhausted from fighting. Every day was a battle, and a large part of him wanted only peace.

When he was younger he'd been certain that he never

wanted to die, but now he felt death calling to him. He was old, he was broken down, and above all he was tired. Sleep did not replenish him. Nothing seemed to. The only way he would find peace now was beneath the blanket of eternal night. He hoped death was as quiet as he imagined it to be.

He thought that, sipped his coffee, looked at Teresa – and looking at her his longing for death faded away. Maybe that was what good love was: a raft that kept you afloat when you would otherwise sink, when you were too exhausted to swim on your own. That was why loss of love was so difficult. You had to learn to start kicking again, and you grew so weary of keeping your head above water that you simply wanted to breathe liquid.

You grew so fucking *weary*.

'What are you thinking?'

He looked at Teresa, at the sober sparkle in her eyes. He hadn't seen it for so long that until it returned he hadn't even realized he had missed it. He had missed her. But now she was back. She was actually present in the room with him for the first time in years.

'Nothing,' he said.

3

Andrew sat in the passenger seat of his father's car while his father drove. A pair of fishing poles jutted from the rear window. A tackle box rested on the backseat, as well as a small cooler filled with liverwurst sandwiches and beer. He glanced over at the man and thought about putting a bullet through his brain.

He pictured it.

He raises the gun in his hand and puts it against his father's temple. He thumbs back the hammer. His heart beats rapidly in his chest. Hatred and anger well up within him, working into his throat from his gut. He can taste their bitterness. He squeezes the trigger. The driver side window shatters as the bullet hammers through it, taking with it blood and brain and shards of bone. The car swerves, crashes into the side of a building. Andrew opens the passenger side door and steps from the vehicle. He walks away. Behind him he can hear a woman screaming. He'll go to prison for what he's done, he knows that, but he doesn't care. He is free – he is finally free of his father. He has finally shed that skin. The anger has left him, the hatred, and he is left with calm in his center, like a quiet country night where the only sound is that of crickets chirping.

He leaned down and turned on the radio.

He looked out the window. The city passed by in a blur.

4

Harry and Andrew sat in fold-out chairs on the shore of Patoka Lake, the cooler between them. They each had a beer propped between their legs and poles in their hands.

Harry thought he'd felt a few nibbles, but hadn't been able to hook anything. He wished this felt like he wanted it to feel, wished it felt relaxed and natural. Instead it felt forced. All he could think about was what might be going through Andrew's head. The boy was here for a reason, and that reason was not simply to get to know him.

In fact, Harry suspected his plans might be violent.

Why not? Despite saying that he believed what Harry had told him he still clearly thought that his father was responsible for his mother's death. It was in his face. It was in his eyes.

But if he did plan to commit a violent act, when was he going to make his move?

'I've been thinking.'

Harry turned to look at his son. 'About what?'

'Rathbone.'

'What about him?'

'Is he still alive?'

Harry nodded. 'He'd be about seventy-five now.'

Andrew looked out at the water, reeled in some of his line.

'Why?'

'I think we should kill him.'

'You – what?'

'If he's responsible for my mother's death, if it all leads back to him and decisions he made, I want the motherfucker dead.'

'He's an old man.'

'I don't care.'

Harry knew what he meant. He'd thought about Rathbone many times in the last twenty-six years. He wanted the man to pay. There'd been times when he almost made it happen, when he almost went back to Dallas simply to finish things once and for all. But then he thought about his quiet life, his peaceful life – sad as it may seem to some on the outside it was everything to him – and realized he didn't want to jeopardize it in order only to have vengeance on a man who probably would not even understand the very human motivation behind his actions.

He was also afraid of once more becoming Harry Combs.

And killing the man would do nothing to better the world. Another one just like him would only step into his place.

Yes – but this one was responsible for Helen's death.

He told himself that but did not believe it. He'd told himself that for years and had *never* believed it. The only one responsible for Helen's death was him. He'd lived the life he'd lived, and she'd died as a result of it.

If anyone should die it was him. And despite what Andrew said Harry was beginning to believe his son intended to make it happen. He believed that getting him to Dallas was part of the boy's plan. All Harry had to do to stop it happening – to stop it happening in the way the boy intended anyway – was to say no.

The question was, would he?

He didn't know. He knew he should. He knew that deep down he didn't even believe Rathbone was responsible. But it was someone on whom to heap his hatred. He could either continue to direct it inward or he could put it on Rathbone and destroy it with a bullet. There was something he liked about the thought. He didn't know if it was realistic. He didn't know if anything could destroy the hatred he had for himself, or the guilt that fed it. But he could try.

He had to try.

If that was what he would actually be doing. A large part of him suspected he would actually be succumbing to his self-loathing rather than trying to destroy it. He would be succumbing to it by giving Andrew just what he wanted. Succumbing to it by knowingly walking into a trap.

Only his actions there would determine what he was actually doing, and he had no idea what his actions would be. He had no idea at all.

Then there was the question of what Andrew was becoming. He'd thought what happened yesterday had sated any hunger for the death the boy might have, but he had been wrong. He believed he had been wrong. The boy still felt murder in his heart. And that's what it was, wasn't it? Yesterday his son had tried to assassinate a man, but assassination was not what he really wanted to do. He lusted for murder, plain and simple.

'Okay,' he said finally.

'What does that mean?'

'Maybe it's time to finish this.'

Andrew nodded.

'I think it is.'

THEN:

Harry meets Rathbone three days after his encounter with the suited man in the bar. The suited man, Dan Russell, brings him to a shirt warehouse about noon. They park behind the building and step out of the car. Harry hangs back, letting Russell lead the way. As they walk into the place the man tells him not to be nervous. Until those words were spoken he'd had no idea he had any reason to be, but hearing them makes his stomach go sour.

'Who is this guy?'

'Rathbone?'

'Yeah.'

'You'll see.'

They walk through the warehouse to a set of stairs, then up the stairs to a glass-walled office which looks down on the warehouse and those working in it. A black-haired man sits behind a large desk looking down at the goings-on below.

But when Harry and Russell step into the open doorway

and Russell knocks on the jamb he turns to give them his attention.

'Is this the one you told me about?'

'It is.'

Rathbone gets to his feet. He stands about five-ten, weighs maybe a hundred and seventy pounds. He wears a fine black suit, immaculately tailored, and a hand-painted tie. His face is all angles. His eyes are black as his hair. He appears calm, relaxed, but there is something violent about him even in this motionless state, some turmoil under the skin.

'Come on in,' he says.

The two men walk into the room, approach the desk, and when they do Rathbone puts his hand out to Harry. Harry takes it. The man's hand is dry and rough as sandpaper. His grip is tight, almost painful.

'Mr Russell tells me you might be of some use to us.'

'I hope so.'

'Why is that?'

'I need money.'

Rathbone smiles. 'Money, we have. Now let's discuss what you might do for it.'

Harry takes a seat.

NOW:

1

They walked out of the airport and into the Dallas sun about half past ten, each of them with a piece of luggage gripped in his fist. The day felt very hot to Andrew after hours on an air-conditioned plane, and he could feel sweat begin to bead on his skin within seconds. His father lighted a cigarette, took a drag.

'Let's get our rental car,' his father said through a cloud of cigarette smoke.

They got a small Toyota, threw their bags into the backseat, and drove to a Motel 6 about twenty minutes away. His father did not reference a map or ask for directions. He seemed to know the area well, despite his long absence.

They got adjoining rooms, his father paying for both of them, and after watching the old man disappear behind a brown door – spend ten minutes washing the flight off, then be ready to head out; there are things we need to take care of – Andrew stepped through his own and locked it behind him both deadbolt and chain. The room was small and smelled of cigarette smoke. The carpet was stained in several places. The lone picture on the wall hung crookedly and there was something desperately sad about it though it was merely of flowers in a vase.

Andrew dropped his duffel bag by the front door, walked to the bed, sat down. He stared at the wall. It had once been white but was now nicotine yellow. He thought about what he would be doing here in Dallas and wondered how exactly it would happen, what he would feel when it was finished. He imagined it would be a great relief, like a weight being lifted off your chest after a very long time, air finally being able to fill your non-constricted lungs, but he could not be certain of that. He wouldn't know until it was over.

All he could be certain of was his need to do it. Nothing else seemed to matter.

Well – soon he *would* do it. Soon it would be finished.

He walked to the bathroom to take a leak.

2

Harry looked at himself in the mirror. He turned on the hot water, waited till steam was rising from the basin, splashed it on his face, dried off with a hand towel. His skin felt thin and raw, as if the towel might simply wipe it off to reveal musculature and bone. He didn't know what he was doing here. He couldn't believe he'd come back. He knew he shouldn't have. It was over. He had a new life with a new woman, a woman he loved, yet he was still letting what happened over a quarter century ago control him. He was letting it control him despite his knowing better, despite knowing that this was something he should leave alone. Every step he took with Andrew was leading him further down a road he'd told himself long ago he'd no longer travel. He should turn back now, turn back and head home to his wife whom he loved and Harry White whom he would much rather be. He did not like the coldness which had begun to flow through his veins. He did not like the small mannerisms which were returning, reminding him every day that he was once more becoming Harry Combs, a man he despised; he did not like the return of his old way of thinking, the combined numbness and self-hatred.

Teresa didn't like it either. Before he left Louisville she had told him she knew where he was going. I know where you're going and I know what you're doing. You don't have to say a word. After more than twenty years I know you as well as you know yourself. You're making a mistake, and I think you know you are. You don't want to do this. You don't want to let this happen to you.

Nothing's going to happen to me.

He told her that before walking out the door. But he didn't believe it.

Less than a minute later they were heading to the airport.

He tossed the hand towel to the counter and walked out of the bathroom.

He sat on the edge of the bed and picked up the telephone. He wiped the earpiece off on his pants, then put it to his ear and dialed information. After three rings a woman picked up, asked him in a sharp voice what city and state.

'Dallas, Texas.'

'Go ahead, sir.'

'The number for Solid Gold Pawn Shop, please.'

She gave him the number and he wrote it down on a note pad.

'Thank you.'

He hung up the phone with his finger, waited a few seconds, and removed the pressure. He dialed the number, surprised the place was still in business. That it was still in business however did not mean Jeff Allen was still running it. Even thirty years ago the man had been a stick of dynamite ready to explode – and dynamite gets more volatile with age, not less.

'What?' The voice was nasally, the word shot out like a bullet.

'Allen?'

'Who's askin?'

'Harry Combs.'

'That's a name I never thought I'd hear again without it being preceded by a curse.'

'Then it's motherfucking Harry Combs.'

A laugh, which stopped abruptly – then: 'Harry Combs is dead.'

'Anybody ever find his body?'

'You never find the body when a man died right.'

'Then consider this his rebirth.'

'You're really Harry Combs?'

'I am.'

'Where you been all this time?'

'The question is who I've been, and I'm not answering.'

Allen laughed his strange laugh. 'Can't say as I blame you.'

'I didn't think you would.'

'You back in town?'

'For a few days. I have some business to attend to.'

'What kinda business?'

'That's what I'm calling about. I need some guns. Long-range rifle with a scope, needs to be accurate up to five hundred yards. Also a couple handguns. I don't care what kind so long as they've got some kick and they aren't garbage.'

'What the hell you need guns for?'

'What, did you pick up a moral compass at the pawnshop?'

'No, nothin like that. Call it simple curiosity.'

'Call it what you want, it's not a question a man in your line of work needs to be asking.'

'Point taken.'

'Can you get me the guns?'

'The rifle will take a few hours.'

'That's fine.'

'Swing by around four.'

'I'll see you then.' Harry hung up the telephone.

He knew that by buying guns from Allen he was also informing Rathbone of his presence in town, but he'd been gone a long time and didn't know who else to call to get the things he needed. It almost made him miss the old days when he could do a hit without his man knowing he was coming. Things were simpler back then.

The good thing about Allen in this situation, however, was that his greed would prevent him from informing Rathbone of Harry's presence until after the guns were sold and collected. The man would not take money out of his own pocket for anybody, and that meant Harry would get what he needed, which was all he cared about at this point.

Well – it wasn't *quite* all he cared about.

He thought about Teresa and wondered if he'd ever see her again. He hoped so. When he thought of himself dead he felt a great loneliness at never getting to hold her in his arms again. He knew if he was dead he'd almost certainly feel nothing, be nothing, but it was hard for him to imagine that. What he imagined was himself in darkness, consciousness without form, lonely and isolated and longing for this woman he loved. And he found that the woman he loved was Teresa White, formerly Teresa Pemberton. When he thought of himself lonely it was her absence he thought of, not Helen's. When he felt hollow inside he knew it was her who could fill him.

Yet if he died, if Andrew did to him what he was afraid the boy intended to do, he knew also that he had it coming.

Well, in the next day or two he'd know what was going to happen.

Or he'd know nothing.

He got to his feet and walked to his duffel bag, which was resting on the suitcase stand in the corner. He unzipped it. He wanted to finish cleaning himself up before heading back out into the day. He felt grimy.

3

Andrew was sitting up in bed watching the local news when someone tapped out 'Shave and a Haircut' on his door. He got to his feet and walked to it. He pulled it open. His father stood on the other side expressionless. He'd changed clothes and brushed his hair.

'You ready?'

'What are we doing?'

His father lit a cigarette, took a drag, and turned toward the car without answering.

Fifteen minutes later they were driving into a mall parking garage. They rolled slowly through the various levels, down and down further underground, his father scanning the vehicles on either side. Finally his father stopped the car. He reached into the inside pocket of his gray sweater and removed a screwdriver. He held it out toward Andrew.

'Get the plate off that Toyota.'

'What?'

'The license plate.'

Andrew took the screwdriver and stepped from the vehicle. He walked to a white Toyota parked between a Ford pickup truck and a large Buick. He looked left, then right. He sat on his haunches and began unscrewing the plate, feeling a nervous sickness in his stomach. But soon enough it was done and no one had seen him or said a word. He walked with the license plate back to the car and fell into the passenger seat.

'Good.'

His father put the car into gear and they drove toward the exit. His father gave the attendant his ticket and a single dollar bill.

A moment later they rolled out into the sun.

Their next stop was a brick warehouse which sat amongst many other brick warehouses on a time-faded street the color of dirty laundry water. The gutters were littered with paper-sacked beer cans, paper cups, discarded shoes, Coca-Cola cans, crushed cigarette packs, and other refuse. Several orange-booted cars, old Buicks and Lincolns mostly, were parked at the curbs, untouched for years it seemed. Several of the warehouses had shattered and boarded-up windows.

They drove past their warehouse, the facade painted with white lettering which read RATHBONE FINE SHIRTS, and at the next corner turned right.

His father pulled the car to the curb and put it into park. He turned and looked toward Andrew. His eyes were red and tired-looking. His face was free of emotion.

'I need to do something.'

'What?'

'Just wait here.'

His father pushed open the door and stepped from the car. He shambled across the street and down an alley to the warehouse's back door.

He disappeared into it.

4

Harry stood in the doorway to the shirt warehouse. He'd not been here in decades, and never really thought he'd return, but here he was. He looked up to the glass-walled office on the second floor to see Rathbone sitting behind his desk. He was nearly bald now, and his shoulders were slumped by time, but it was him all right. Harry knew it would be. He'd made enquiries. But he'd also wanted to see it for himself; he'd needed to see it for himself.

Somehow it was like looking at the face of God. His entire life had been shaped by this man, and time had turned him into a shadow, a myth. He'd become a symbol for everything that had gone wrong in Harry's life. He was not a real man. He had ceased to be a real man long ago.

Except he *was* a real man, wasn't he? One cannot kill a shadow.

It was strange to think that twenty-six years ago he'd been running from Rathbone and today he had walked right through his door. Time changed things.

Everything that happened back then, it felt like it'd happened to someone else.

Before anyone could even turn to look at him, he pushed his way out into the Dallas sunshine. He lighted a cigarette. He looked toward the rental car, but once more turned away from it. His business here was not done. He still needed to find his perch.

Soon enough he had.

5

Andrew sat at the table across from his father and took a bite of his tuna fish sandwich. It was bland as elevator music, seemed not to have been seasoned at all, but that didn't matter much. There probably wasn't a meal in the world he could relax and enjoy today, not with what was on his mind. He merely needed sustenance, fuel for the machine that was his body.

'What's the plan exactly?'

'We take him tomorrow.'

'That soon?'

'I don't see any reason to wait. We know where he'll be. We know he has to walk from his car to the warehouse. We have a good location from which to shoot. A getaway vehicle can be parked nearby. We take care of it in the morning, we can be on a plane by noon.'

'Makes sense,' Andrew said. But he knew only one of them would be getting on a plane tomorrow, only one of them would be walking away at all. He felt sick when he thought about it, but he also felt a strange excitement. It was finally going to be over; he was finally going to be rid of his father. He would finally shed that skin in order that he might become – once and for all – completely himself. 'What preparations do we have left to make today?'

His father shook his head. 'We have to pick up a few

things,' he said, 'but that's all. We'll switch the plates tomorrow morning before we head out.'

The old man butted out his cigarette in the half sandwich remaining on his plate.

6

Harry pulled the rental car into the pawnshop's parking lot, shoved the transmission handle forward till it locked, and killed the engine. He looked toward Andrew. Andrew looked back, and after a moment Harry saw something flash behind his eyes. He didn't know what it meant, but it was something.

He ignored it – simply let it go – and said: 'I'll be back in ten minutes.'

Andrew nodded.

Harry stepped from his vehicle. He pulled up his pants. He lighted a cigarette and inhaled. He stood there smoking until the thing was burned down to its filter. He thought about tomorrow and what it meant, what it might mean.

This would be his first out-and-out assassination since November 1963. He'd killed people since then, of course, but those were acts of self-defense – acts of self-preservation, anyway. Tomorrow would be different. Tomorrow would be a straightforward assassination, and there was simply no way around it.

He wondered if allowing Harry Combs back so fully was wise. He wondered whether he'd be able to banish him if he did. It might be more difficult this time. If he allowed Harry Combs to take over completely, as he would have to do, it might be impossible to push him out again. He believed he could do it now, but tomorrow?

He simply wasn't sure.

He flicked his butt away and walked toward the pawn-shop.

He pushed through the door and at the other end of the room, beyond all the second-hand products, tools and lamps and guitars and chairs, saw a small man with thin blond hair standing behind a glass case filled with cheap jewelry.

The man turned toward him when the door's bell rang. For a moment his eyes were blank as an elementary school's chalkboards during summer vacation, then he recognized the man who'd stepped through his door.

'I'll be goddamned,' the man said.

'Most of us will.'

'I know we talked, but I never expected you to walk through my door.'

'I warned you I was coming.'

'Even so. I feel like I'm looking at a ghost.'

'Do you have what I need?'

'I have what everybody needs. It's my business. Step into the back with me.'

Harry did.

7

His father knew what he was planning, had probably known for some time. He'd told himself he would act as if that were the case, but he hadn't. He hadn't acted that way because he hadn't believed it, not really. He knew that Teresa didn't trust him, and he knew that she might have told her husband of her mistrust, but what he saw in his father's eyes was knowledge. That, and a very deep sadness.

How far would his father let this go before he finally ended it? He was certain that his father *could* end it. If he knew what was coming – and he did – there was no way Andrew could beat him, no way Andrew could kill him. It was as simple as that.

And yet – he had to try, didn't he?

He had to try because if he didn't he would not be able to live with himself. He would be still full of all this anger and hatred and his failure would add to that regret. It would eat away at him; it would rust his soul. And the thought of that was intolerable. After all he had gone through to get to this point he *had* to follow through.

8

Harry pulled into the motel's parking lot and brought the vehicle to a stop. He stepped out into the sun. He lit a cigarette, and, feeling that he was being watched, glanced left. At the other end of the parking lot sat a green Chrysler Le Baron, and through the glass Harry could see a face. The face was turned toward him.

Was it possible that Rathbone had a man on him already? His heart began thudding heavily in his chest. His mouth went dry.

Then the person in the green Chrysler started the engine. The car backed out of its spot, then rolled through the parking lot toward the street. After traffic cleared it rolled into the street, and a moment later was gone from view. Harry looked toward the place he'd last seen it for several minutes, smoking and thinking, before deciding he was being paranoid. It was nothing.

It had to be nothing.

He flicked his cigarette away and walked to the trunk. He opened the trunk and pulled from within a battered guitar case. He slammed shut the trunk and walked toward his motel room. He was soon to do something about which he had significant doubts.

'Come with me,' he said.

He unlocked his door and stepped into the motel

room. His son followed behind him silent, pensive. They both stepped inside. Harry locked the door, walked to the bed, and set down the guitar case. He unlatched the clasps and swung open the lid. Inside were a rifle and two pistols, all three of them untraceable, as well as several boxes of rounds. He picked up one of the pistols, checked the clip, slid it back into place.

Then he held it out toward Andrew.

Andrew looked from the pistol in his father's hand to his face, hesitated a moment, and took it.

'You shouldn't need it,' Harry said, 'but there's a chance things will get out of hand tomorrow. If they do I want you to have protection.'

'Thank you.'

He tucked the pistol into his pants and covered it with his T-shirt.

'Meet me at the car tomorrow morning, six thirty.'

Andrew nodded. 'I'll be there.'

Then he turned toward the door, opened it, stepped outside.

Harry watched him go, and as the door closed behind him felt a strange tightness in his chest. He loved the boy, wanted nothing more than to have his son *be* his son, but knew that was never going to happen, knew it never *could* happen. Too many things had gone wrong between them – before they even met on equal terms, before Andrew drove out to see him, even then it was too late. By decades.

That relationship was lost.

THEN:

Teresa moves in with him only six weeks after their first meeting. It is strange and wonderful and somehow terrible to be with someone new, to be with someone who makes him happy. He loved Helen, but they'd hurt and betrayed each other. There was nothing clean about their relationship, not by the time it ended. Having happiness now makes him realize how unhappy he once was – he'd had no idea while he was in the middle of it – but it also makes him feel guilty. For he doesn't believe he deserves happiness. He is not a good man, has never been a good man – so how can he deserve happiness and peace?

He knows he cannot, does not.

He deserves Helen, and despite her being gone, a part of him still clings to her. Part of it is love, a love he still feels, but most of it is guilt.

For months, though, he and Teresa are happy together. He manages to push away the guilt and the self-hatred in order to be with her, and she manages to do the same. She drinks too *much when they go out, but most of the time she remains sober, happy simply to be with him as he is with her. But as time progresses, as the months become years, he feels himself sinking back into himself. His guilt overwhelms him, and he pulls away from Teresa knowing that he does not and cannot deserve her, and she must feel it for she begins drinking during the day. Not every day, not at first, but enough that he notices, and he knows that she is drinking so that she can tolerate his presence. If he were fully in the relationship she wouldn't have to – he knows that – but because he has pulled away while remaining with her physically it is painful. He can see it in her eyes. But this only adds to his guilt – he cannot even make someone so deserving of happiness feel happy; he is a waste of skin who cannot give what is required – and this makes him pull back further.*

Sometimes he'll see the loneliness in her eyes and wish he had the courage to leave her; she would be happier without him than she can be with him, for there is nothing lonelier than being lonely in another's presence.

But sometimes they forget themselves. Sometimes they have perfect, pure moments, and those seem to be enough to keep going.

He wishes he were capable of more, he wishes he could simply let go of the past and let it sink into the murky depths, but he cannot. He simply doesn't know how to do it.

Maybe someday.

NOW:

1

Andrew awakened the next morning at six o'clock. He felt groggy after a fitful sleep. He had tossed and turned throughout the night thinking about his father giving him that pistol, wondering why the man would do such a thing if he knew what Andrew was planning. He'd been wondering how he was going to make it happen and his father had handed him an answer, and from the look in his eyes he'd known exactly what he was doing.

It didn't make any sense.

On the surface it didn't. But there were two possibilities that, if true, could provide context for his seemingly nonsensical action. The first was that the man wanted to die, believed he deserved what was coming to him, but that seemed unlikely. It didn't jibe with how Andrew pictured the man. The second was that his father intended to kill him and didn't want to do it while he remained unarmed. Perhaps he could justify it to himself if the act was one of self-defense. A stranger was one thing; his son was another.

Maybe it didn't matter *why* he'd done it. He'd done it. He'd handed his son the gun that was going to kill him.

But of course it mattered. It was important that Andrew know what he was walking into. This wasn't a game. It was life and death. Either he would die today or his father would, and he did not want to die. He wanted to go home to Melissa. He wanted to hold her in his arms. He wanted to awaken in the morning and know that he was free of this man he hated.

More than wanting those things, he needed them.

So he would have to wait for his moment, he would have to wait until he knew it was safe to act, and only then would he do what he needed to do.

He pushed the blankets off his body and rolled out of bed. He walked to the bathroom and turned on the tub, waiting for the water to warm up.

He closed his eyes and imagined killing his father.

As he watched the man drop to the ground he felt peace.

2

With the guitar case in hand Harry stepped into the warm Dallas morning. He walked to the rental car and put the case into the trunk. He lit a cigarette and inhaled deeply. He looked out on the half-empty parking lot and thought about his son. His hope – his only hope – was that the boy would not be able to do it. Maybe he thought he could, but in the moment would he really be able to? The answer had to be no. Harry hoped it did, anyway, because he was going to do nothing to stop it. He felt he had no right. Doing what he was doing today meant he had no right, for the boy was doing exactly the same thing as he was and for the same reason.

Only his target was different.

Harry flicked away his cigarette butt.

He bent down to unscrew the license plate and did so, tossing it into the backseat. He put the stolen plate in its place. He looked at his watch. It was six twenty-eight. Soon they would be on their way.

He lit another cigarette, glanced toward the green Chrysler parked once more at the other end of the lot, and waited for Andrew to emerge.

3

Andrew's father parked the car by the curb and killed the engine. They were about two hundred yards from the warehouse, next to an abandoned building with boarded-up windows and graffiti-covered brick walls. Between this building and the warehouse lay nothing but an empty lot.

Shattered beer bottles and other litter lay amongst the tall brown grass and the weeds.

'Let's get ready,' his father said, pushing open his door.

4

They trudged up creaky steps toward the third floor. Harry walked in front, carrying the guitar case in his right hand. He thought about the gun he'd handed his son and wondered when he might pull it out. The boy was about three steps behind him now, the stairwell was narrow, and Harry was encumbered besides. It would be the perfect moment. He kept expecting it, but it never happened.

They reached the third floor and Harry walked to a wall of boarded-up windows. He looked through cracks in the plywood, trying to find his best angle, his best window, and when he did he tore the plywood away. He looked out through the cracked window to the warehouse beyond. Beside the docks lay the parking area. For the time being it was empty, but as the day progressed it would fill up. Employees would arrive and park and head in to work. Perhaps someone from a retail shop would stop by to talk business. George Rathbone would arrive as well, step from his vehicle, and start walking toward the back door a mere twenty-five feet from where he'd parked.

But of course he'd never make it.

Harry set the guitar case down on the floor and opened it. He removed from within it his rifle, and set himself up a comfortable firing position on the windowsill by breaking away an already cracked pane of glass and pulling over a wooden chair.

He looked through the scope down to the parking lot. It was about two hundred and fifteen yards away. The breeze was mild. He exhaled. It had been a very long time since he'd done anything like this. He had to be focused. He had to make the first shot count. If he missed and Rathbone heard the report, the man would be gone in a second, for if he was anything he was a survivor. Which meant Harry could not miss. He was tempted to go for a body shot, to increase the size of his target, but unless he hit just right the man might still be mobile. No – he'd have to go for the head first. Or maybe he'd pop off two in quick succession. With the first he'd take his time, control his breathing, go for the head. The second he'd get off right after, one for the body.

As he thought about this a cold feeling came over him. The nervousness left, as did thoughts about how long it had been. His world became smaller, so small that he could see the whole thing through a single scope mounted on a rifle. This was how it was supposed to be.

But then he once more thought about Andrew.

He opened his left eye and looked at the boy's ghostly reflection in the window. He stood motionless behind Harry, watching.

Finally he said: 'Can I do anything?'

Harry shook his head. 'The only thing left now is to do it.' He turned his head to look at his son. 'The man responsible for your mother's death *will* pay for what he's done.'

'Yes,' Andrew said, 'he will.'

5

Andrew stood behind his father and watched as cars arrived, as men and women stepped from them and walked into the warehouse. He thought about the pistol tucked into the front of his Levi's. He thought about his father standing only five feet away. He felt sick to his stomach, wanted to vomit, but he wouldn't allow himself to vomit. He was going to do this. Unless his father turned on him and put a stop to it he was going to do this. He would release all his anger and hatred in a single round, and that round would pierce the back of his father's skull, would kill him, and it would be over.

Once and for all it would be over.

6

Harry waited for what seemed a very long time. He wanted a cigarette but refused himself one, as he always had while working on a hit. There was no room in him for anything but this one task. He would even have to push thoughts of Andrew out of his head. The boy was going to do it or he wasn't, but thinking about it served no purpose. He desperately wanted to see Teresa again, but if he didn't he wouldn't miss her. The dead don't miss anything. She might miss him, but he couldn't worry about that.

Except he *was* worried about that. He was worried about her. He did not want to abandon her, and allowing this to happen made him feel as if he was doing just that. He was allowing the past to control his present actions, and in so doing he was willingly sacrificing the only true thing in his life – his love for his wife, the woman who had helped to save him from himself.

That was something he'd never told her. He should have, but he never had. Without her he would have been dead a long time ago. She gave him a reason to carry on. She gave him someone besides himself to care about. Even when he was at his most self-loathing, even when he felt worthless and vile, he knew he had her to love and be loved by, and while they were both fucked up in their own ways, the love itself was pure, the purest he'd ever known.

So why was he going to give that up for a mistake he'd made twenty-six years ago? Why was he willing to abandon the only person who'd known him fully – both good and bad – and loved him anyway?

Did he deserve the punishment that he believed Andrew was about to deliver? He thought he very well might. He'd done things most men would never do. He'd killed his wife. He'd abandoned his son. So, yes, he very well might have this coming – except he was not *only* the man who had done those things. He was another man besides, a good man. Wasn't he? He had spent decades living a quiet life, hurting no one, and he had been happy – as happy as he'd ever been – and that part of him, that man within the man, he deserved no punishment.

Rathbone's car rolled down the alley and came to a stop. The driver side door swung open and Rathbone stepped from his vehicle.

'He's here,' Harry said.

'So this is it.'

Harry nodded briefly, and put his eye to the scope. He lined up his target carefully. He slowed his breathing. He brought his index finger from the trigger guard to the trigger itself.

But he could not find focus. He could not make his world shrink again as it should have.

He thought about his son standing behind him. He heard the pistol slide from his son's pants, the cold metal brushing against denim.

He wanted to look into Teresa's eyes again. He wanted to tell her how much she meant to him, how much she had done for him. He didn't think she knew those things. He didn't think she knew that she had saved his life. He wanted to tell her those things, but he also wanted finally to pay for his crimes.

That was it, wasn't it? He was fighting the currents of contradictory feelings swimming within him. He was two men, and the one he hated, the one he despised – well, he wanted that son of a bitch to pay almost as much as his son did. He was certain of it. For no matter how much his son hated him, he hated himself equally as much.

Yet here he was about to hand himself over to that man, about to hand himself over to Harry Combs – and for mere vengeance and nothing more. Yes, he wanted it – he wanted it so badly he could taste it like bile in the back of his mouth – but he was not certain it was worth the cost.

If he was going to die today he wanted to die clean, as clean as a man such as him *could* die, anyway. Yes, he had done bad things in the last two weeks. He had killed. But those kills were made in self-defense. His life had been threatened. Everything he loved had been threatened. This was a different thing altogether, and if he actually went through with it he would no longer be the man he had worked so hard to become. He would die not as Harry White but as Harry Combs. Maybe nobody else would know that, but he would. He would know, and that was enough. He could not do this. He could not allow himself this final corruption. It simply wasn't worth it. It had never been worth it.

He pulled his eye away from the scope. He looked into the window's glass.

Andrew was standing behind him, gun drawn.

It was aimed directly at the back of Harry's head.

He was so focused on his son's reflection in the glass that he did not see the green Chrysler pull to the curb three storeys below.

THEN:

He holds Andrew in his arms for the first time only hours after his birth. He can barely believe that a man as awful as he could help to create such a beautiful boy, pure and innocent and red in the face.

'I love you,' he says as he cradles the tiny thing in his arms. 'I love you and I won't ever let anything bad happen to you. I promise.'

NOW:

1

Andrew wraps his hand around the pistol's grip and pulls it from his waistband. The metal is cool against his palm, the pistol heavy. He raises his arm and points it at the back of his father's head. This is the son of a bitch who killed his mother, the son of a bitch who abandoned him. This is the evil bastard who did those things and he is his son. He looks like him. He sounds like him. He walks like him. He wants so badly to be free of him. He needs to be free of him. If he kills the man maybe the similarities within him will die too. Maybe then he might become himself.

He has to do it. He must.

He closes his eyes and exhales. He opens his eyes. He's going to do it. He can feel it building within him, a great pressure, and he knows he really is going to do it.

Is this real?

He doesn't know; he doesn't care.

For the first time in his life he is training a pistol on his father's head and knows that he will act upon his urge. Even in earlier fantasies he was unable to act, but now it's coming on. Now it's happening.

He will wait until his father pulls the trigger on his rifle, and in the same moment he will pull his own. He will end this. He will be free.

He will be free.

He will be—

His father leans back, pulling away from his rifle. He turns his head. Their eyes meet.

The man is so sad. His eyes are moist and wide.

He looks so kind, somehow beautiful in his kindness.

But that is a lie. It's a goddamn lie. He knows it is. He knows it is because he knows what the man is capable of, knows what he's already done. He doesn't care about the son of a bitch's eyes. He doesn't care about anything but this hatred within him, this rage. He must be free of it. He must finally be free of it.

He's going to pull the trigger. He can feel it happening. The pressure against the tip of his finger increases, the metal of the trigger putting a dent into his skin. Then the trigger begins to move, begins to—

'You don't have to do this.'

'You don't know anything about me.'

2

'I know you hate me,' Harry said. 'I know you hate me and you blame me for your mother's death – and you're not wrong to hate me. But this isn't the way.'

Even as he spoke those words he knew they would do no good. The boy was no longer there. His eyes were distant and dreamy. Even the way he spoke sounded dreamy, as if he were talking in his sleep.

This was the face of the man who was going to kill him: his own son.

He thought of Teresa. He wanted to see her again. He wanted to tell her all the things he'd never told her but should have. He was going to die and knowing this he thought not of Helen who had kept him distant from his new wife even in death but of Teresa. He'd made her life miserable for years, he'd made her lonely even in his presence, and all because of his guilt. He wanted to make it right. He wanted to love her in the way she deserved to be loved. He wanted to give to her all of himself.

But now that he realized this he was not going to have the chance.

'Harry?'

He looked toward the sound of her voice.

Teresa emerged from the darkness of the stairwell. An automatic pistol hung from her right hand. It was his pistol, the one he kept in the safe in his library.

He was losing his mind. He was seeing what he wanted to see.

She looked from him to Andrew. She raised the pistol.

'Put the gun down,' she said.

'Are you really here?'

She didn't answer. Instead she said: 'Put it down, Andrew.'

3

Andrew turns his head at the sound of a woman's voice. The cunt his father married stands not fifteen feet away with a gun in her hand. The gun is aimed at his face. He doesn't care. He doesn't care at all. She can shoot him if she wants to, but he'll shoot his father first. He'll die free. That's all that matters to him right now.

'I will not put it down.'

He turns away from her, looks at his father once more.

'You know what you've done,' he says. 'You know you have this coming.'

'I do,' his father says, 'you're right. But please – please don't do this.'

'It's done.'

Andrew puts pressure against the trigger and feels the trigger move.

A shot rings out.

4

Harry flinched at the sound of the report and closed his eyes. Something warm and wet splashed against his face. Then everything went very quiet. He opened his eyes and was not dead. He looked at Teresa. Smoke wafted from the barrel of her gun. He looked at Andrew. The front of his shirt was torn away and there was a hole in his chest big enough to put your fist into.

The boy fell to his knees.

5

The gun kicks in his hand. His father's head is slammed back by the bullet's impact, slammed into the window.

Glass shatters.

Then his body slumps. His head droops down. Blood trickles from the hole in his forehead, drips onto his khaki pants. His eyes are open but lifeless as glass.

He did it.

He fucking did it.

He is finally free. He is finally free.

In his joy he drops to his knees. He has finally managed to shed his father's skin. He is finally able to become himself.

He is free!

6

The boy fell to his side and let go of the pistol. His breathing slowed. He stared at Harry with glassy eyes and opened his mouth to speak.

'I got you – you son of a bitch,' he said.

Then he said no more.

Harry looked from his son to his wife. Her eyes were wide.

'He was going to kill you.'

'I know.'

'You didn't deserve that.'

He begins to cry. 'But I did. I wanted to see you again. You were all I could think about. But I did deserve it. I did.'

'You didn't kill Helen. You didn't make your son what he became. I know what happened. You *know* I know what happened. You've already paid plenty, Harry. Don't you realize that? You've paid enough.'

THEN:

Harry pushes himself off the floor, blood seeping from the bullet hole in his head. He looks over to Helen who lies dead on the floor. Then he looks past flames to his son – to the boy he has raised as his son – screaming in his crib. He has to get out of here. He has to get both himself and his son out of here before the whole place is consumed and the two of them with it.

He grabs his automatic pistol from the nightstand and tucks it into his pants.

He walks through the flames toward his son. His head throbs with pain, throbs to the beat of his heart. And part of him can't believe his heart is still beating. He picks the boy up and looks once more toward Helen.

How is his heart still beating when he knows it's broken?

He has been surprised many times by human resilience. There are suicides, of course, but mostly life wants to go on living. He is no different.

A broken heart can go on beating indefinitely.

He turns toward the door. He knows he must make his way through it. He must get out of this room, and then out of this house.

But something in the doorway is blocking his path. No, not something – someone. Paul Watkins stands there, briefcase in hand.

'You came back for the boy.'

'He's my son.'

Harry shakes his head.

Paul Watkins looks to the floor, to his revolver lying on it, surrounded by flames.

'You should make sure a job is done before throwing your tools away,' Harry says as he takes aim with the automatic.

'I'll see you on the other side,' Paul Watkins says.

'You should know better than that.'

Harry squeezes the trigger, and Paul Watkins drops to the floor.

NOW:

Harry wiped at his eyes and looked toward Teresa. She stood there in a white cotton dress with that same pistol hanging from her right hand. She was sober. She was beautiful. She had saved him for the second time. Somehow looking at her as she stood there like that he felt as if he were looking at her for the very first time. He loved her more now than he ever had, and he'd always loved her more than he'd loved anyone else. Despite the mistakes, despite the guilt he had clung to and the distance he had kept because of that guilt, he loved her wholly, and somehow, for reasons he didn't even understand, he was capable of feeling it wholly, with nothing between it and him, with nothing between Teresa and him.

Then he looked once more at his son. The boy lay on the wooden floor lifeless.

It shouldn't have had to happen that way, but it had. Either Harry had to die or the boy did, and while Harry felt a great sadness at the loss of what might have been – if only Andrew had been able to forgive him, if only he'd not allowed himself to be controlled by rage and by hatred – he knew that ifs didn't matter.

He understood that now more than ever.

He'd spent decades dwelling on ifs when all the time he'd had what could be a wonderful reality right in front of him. He'd made himself miserable and he'd made Teresa miserable by living in moments that had already happened and that could never change.

He was done with that.

He would waste no more years. Maybe he and Teresa didn't have too many more in front of them, he didn't know, but he was going to live them. He was going to be present in them and feel them and appreciate them for what they were.

He got to his feet and walked toward Teresa. He wrapped his arms around her and put his face into her neck and inhaled her scent.

He held her more tightly in his arms than he'd ever held anyone, and while he felt a great sadness inside, he also felt something like joy. He was an old man, an old man whose life was filled with regrets, an old man whose life had for the most part been wasted, but he finally knew just where he belonged. He finally knew just who he was. Harry Combs was dead. Harry Combs had died while sitting at that window with a rifle in his hands.

He'd asked Teresa only minutes ago if she was really

here. She was, and so was he. His name was Harry White and he was a good man. He was a gentle man. He'd once been someone else but that someone else was dead.

It was time to let go of the dead.

AN INTERVIEW WITH
RYAN DAVID JAHN

1. The excerpts from the CIA manual on assassinations
    are chilling – were they based on any real
    information you found during your research?

They're slightly edited excerpts from an actual CIA manual
on assassination, and when I say slightly edited I mean it:
they're *almost* unaltered. I discovered this manual when
I was sixteen or seventeen, I don't remember how, and it
stuck with me, so when I started working on this novel I
knew I wanted to include it. I find its matter-of-fact tone
disturbing but somehow appropriate to the subject matter.

2. In the novel there is the implication that Harry
    Combs was involved in the assassination of JFK in
    1963. Do you have any particular theories on what
    happened?

I think Jack Ruby's murder of Oswald means that we will never know exactly why he assassinated Kennedy, but I'm fairly certain he, in fact, did, and that he acted alone. Oswald had months earlier attempted to assassinate another man. He wanted to do something that would be remembered after his death, and rather than an act of creation he chose destruction, which tends, historically, to work out just as well – often better. The implication in the novel is pure fiction and has nothing whatsoever to do with any real-life theories I might have.

3. **What were the challenges (research, literary, psychological, and logistical) in bringing the story to life?**

The main difficulty was in externalizing what is, really, an internal story. This is, at its heart, a quiet tale about a father–son relationship which just happens to take the form of a thriller. I wanted the motives of both main characters to be clear without beating them into the ground. The actions of the main characters are not logical in the way that is often expected in thrillers; they are based on emotion, which rarely has anything to do with logic. Yet I wanted them to be understood and to make internal sense.

4. **Harry's relationships appear quite dysfunctional, yet they seem to work. Was it difficult to write such**

troubled characters and are any of them remotely autobiographical?

Troubled characters are the only kind I really know how to write. I don't know how normal, happy people think. That is completely alien to me. So in that sense every character is autobiographical. But more specifically, I went through a period during which I was very afraid of becoming my own father, a troubled alcoholic and drug addict who ended up killing himself in the small trailer in which he lived in Bullhead City, Arizona (which is where I got the name for Bulls Mouth, Texas, in *The Dispatcher*). I have his voice, many of his mannerisms, and both his depressive tendencies and violent streak. But I, of course, am not him. Each man lives the life he makes for himself. Destiny, as a concept, is a dead end.

5. What inspired you to write your first book?

I've been writing since I was twelve, and when you grow up writing it eventually becomes a part of who you are. Writing is as fundamental as sex. So I wrote the first book simply because writing is what I do, and I chose that concept because when I rifled through my brain the day I sat down to write, that one seemed the ripest. It was ready to be written. In fact it was probably overripe. I finished the first draft in about a week, and it was almost all there. I haven't written a book that quickly since.

6. What makes crime/thrillers so fascinating for you?

I'm married to a woman whom I love with all my heart. I have two beautiful little girls at home. I live in a nice house on a quiet street and drive a car with three thousand miles on it. But I don't understand my neighbors. I understand poverty and desperation and criminal intent. I understand the rage which might drive a man to murder. And, since my father killed himself and my first wife died of breast cancer, I understand death both quick and protracted, and I understand that what might appear to be a quick death is in fact usually protracted, the conclusion of a long struggle of an emotional nature rather than a physical one. I understand the consequences of death for those left behind. I might be able to write a suburban novel about parenthood, that is the world in which I now live, but I'd have very little to say about it. I do, on the other hand, have something to say about violence and loss, about the stress of having no rent money and only a gun by which to attain it. Crime fiction allows me to talk about the things that interest me, and more, about the things I have some genuine understanding of.

7. Many of your books seem to be connected to the 1950s and 1960s. What draws you to that period of history?

Part of my use of that era is necessity. *The Last Tomorrow*, for instance, has a subplot involving a district attorney attempting to indict the creators of a comic book for negligent homicide, as their work inspired a murder. Such an indictment would never happen today, but in the 1950s, when books were regularly burned and banned, it would have been a possibility. It also happens to be the last era to which today's America still feels historically connected, and you can draw lines both further into the past from there, and forward, toward the present. Slavery, for instance, feels like it happened a very long time ago to most people, but there are men and women walking around today who remember when they couldn't eat at the counter in Woolworth's, and those same people might have had great-grandparents who were slaves.

8. Have you ever been in trouble with the police?

I've been on the verge of trouble a number of times, but I happen to be very polite and fairly clean-cut – I'm thirty-five but could still pass for an earnest undergrad – which means I have gotten away with things that I had no right to get away with. I've had encounters with the police, but those encounters have resulted in nothing more than a few words, and once in some confiscated dope, which is to say, the police have generally been kind to me. Yet I do not trust them.

9. Are there any stories you've wanted to tell, but
    haven't yet been able to?

Of course. But I'll get to them.

10. Where do you find the inspiration for your novels?

Life, news items, eavesdropping on conversations, idle
thoughts: stories can come from anywhere, and usually do.

11. Who is your favorite author?

No such beast exists. Stephen King made me want to be a
writer, but I see many more of his flaws these days (which
didn't stop me from blatantly stealing structural elements
of *From a Buick 8* for this novel; I'll cheerfully take whatever is useful from any and every writer I read, and, short
of plagiarism, think every other writer should do the same).
Dostoyevsky's *Notes from Underground* did for me what
Catcher in the Rye was supposed to. *Moby Dick* is so good
it makes me feel hopeless about my own writing. Cormac
McCarthy is probably the most important writer working in
America today, but he isn't necessarily the most enjoyable.
There are writers for every mood, and being mercurial, as
soon as I picked a favorite my mind would change.

12. If you could offer aspiring thriller writers one piece
    of advice, what would it be?

If you're able to do it, write a series. This is my fifth standalone novel, and every time a new book comes out I feel as though I'm starting over. Those who liked the last book might have no interest in this one while those who read but hate this one might, in fact, enjoy the next. Series have a built-in audience. Each book is an advertisement for the next, and each book is similar enough to the last that the audience you carry with you will probably like each subsequent one. That is an excellent position to put yourself in career-wise. That said, a career as a novelist is uncertain for all but the most successful of us, financially speaking, so as soon as you sell a novel, buy yourself a bottle of antacids; it can be hell on the stomach.

extracts reading groups
competitions books new
discounts extracts
competitions
books
new
events books
extracts
new books
reading groups
interviews
events extracts
discounts
new books events
events new
reading groups
events
books
interviews
discounts extracts discounts
www.panmacmillan.com
extracts events reading groups
competitions books extracts new
books